MW01132570

THE CONUNDRUM OF COLLIES

A Love & Pets Romantic Comedy, Book 6

A.G. HENLEY

CENTRAL PARK BOOKS

This is a work of fiction. Names, characters, places, and incidents are the product of the author's imagination or are used fictitiously. Any resemblance to actual person, living or dead, events, or locales is entirely coincidental.

Text copyright © 2020 by A.G. Henley

Cover Designed by Najla Qamber Designs (www.najlaqamberdesigns.com)

All rights reserved by A. G. Henley

Visit me at aghenley.com

Summary: Two best friends teeter on the edge of love and friendship, accompanied by an energetic border collie.

CONTENTS

Hey, readers!

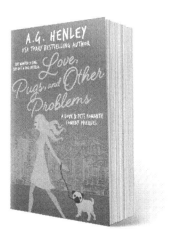

Get the FREE prequel ebook to the Love & Pets series, *Love, Pugs, and Other Problems,* an exclusive short story that tells how Amelia gets Doug the pug instead of a ring!

Chapter One

Stevie

Sitting at my desk in my bedroom, I put the finishing touches on a logo for a freelance client. I take a last look at the the work, stick the files into Dropbox, and pop the link into an email thanking him for his business.

The client, Choppy Carter, the beer-bellied and mustachioed owner of a pool and hot tub cleaning and repair company called Wet & Wild, wanted to "update" his company's image. The previous logo was a cartoon illustration of a blonde, busty, bikini clad lady leaning out of a hot tub. It was wet and wild, all right, but several clients had complained in recent years, and he felt he was losing business.

After a month of going back and forth with Choppy, I finally persuaded him to narrow down his choices to one tasteful and minimal design using two uppercase Ws and an ampersand that can be easily applied to everything from his invoices to his trucks. Now, the logo is finished, and he's paid in full, so that should be that. A good day's work.

I stretch my arms in the air and look around. "Bean? Beanie Weenie? Where are you?"

Wincing at the pain in my lower back from sitting too long, I twist from side to side as I walk out of my bedroom, also known as my office, down the hall and into the tiny bungalow kitchen, looking for my three-year-old border collie, Bean. Usually, she's asleep on or beside my bed while I work. The fact that she's not right now probably means trouble.

"Logan? Is Bean with you?" I ask my best friend and roommate who's shooting someone in the living room. In a video game, that is.

"What?" he yells back.

I roll my eyes and shout my question louder. He wears headphones, so he never hears me the first time I say something.

"No," he finally answers. "Uh oh, did she get out?"

"I don't know. Bean?" I call her again.

If she were in the house, I'd hear the clicking of her toenails against our worn wooden floors, coming to me. I don't hear them. The back door shudders as I yank it open and poke my head out into the yard. It's early June and unusually misty and cool today. I shiver.

"Bean?"

Nothing. No streak of black and white fur as my girl rushes across the overgrown, weedy yard to my side. My heart stutters with panic and then sinks. Did she get into Rosa's yard again? I hear a shrill bark from next door, followed by a great deal of terrified squawking. Yeah, she did.

I run to my room to grab my black hoodie off the back of my desk chair and shove my feet into my white Converse low top shoes, shouting to Logan at the same time. "Bean's next door again!"

"What?" He pulls one ear pad off his ear as I careen from the hall to the kitchen door again.

"Bean. Rosa. Chickens!"

"I'm right behind you!"

Dodging our worn patio furniture, I sprint to the gate in our wood fence, throw it open, and dart inside our neighbor Rosa's yard. I hurry to the chicken coop in back and stop short. I really, really hope Rosa's still at work and not seeing this.

Her ten backyard hens huddle together in a corner of their pen. The poor things squawk, flap their wings, and their already buggy eyes seem extra buggy as my border collie menace does her best to herd them. Not that they understand her intentions. As far as the hens are concerned, Bean's pointy white teeth, set into a horrifying slash of a barking mouth, are bent on death and destruction. The chickens can't know that herding and chasing are in my dog's blood, and when she sees their plump, wingy bodies, she can't help but *encourage* them to stay all together. Her instinct is inevitable. So is the hens' fear. They scatter.

"Bean! Come!" I shout the command as Logan jogs up beside me. He claps to get her attention.

My dog glances at us, clearly torn. Herd the chickens, like she'd been born to do, or obey her mistress and that guy who's always around her mistress who sneaks her bites of meat from his plate and takes her on walks? Hmm, choices.

Logan produces a treat from his pocket. Smart. I should have thought to grab one. Showing Bean the incentive, he strolls over and gently takes her collar in hand while she snarfs the biscuit, then he pulls Bean's leash out of his back pocket. Ugh. Smart again. I only thought of my bare feet and arms before running outside instead of grabbing the necessary tools to bring the escapee home.

As Logan hooks the leash on my dog's collar and leads her away from the flock, I swear the chickens' combs and wattles droop with relief. Logan squints apologetically at something—or someone—behind me. I twist around.

"Stevie, I swear, I'm going to call animal control on that dog next time." Rosa's expression is pinched. She wears a navy-blue dress with one sensible heel and one bare foot, like she'd walked in from work and just had time to kick a single shoe off before she'd noticed the commotion in the backyard.

"I'm *so* sorry, Rosa." I take Bean's leash from Logan. "I don't know how she got in here."

"That's what you said last time." Our neighbor eyes Bean. I don't think she dislikes my dog. She wishes she wouldn't terrorize her flock, a totally reasonable desire.

"We boarded up the hole in the fence she was getting through," Logan says.

"Well, obviously she found a new one," Rosa answers in a clipped tone.

"We'll find it and get it patched," I say. "I'm really sorry again. Let me know if any of the hens are hurt. I'll pay the vet bill." Bean doesn't bite them, but sometimes in their panic to get away from her, they peck each other, causing injuries.

"Trust me, I will," Rosa says.

I sigh. I don't blame her for being upset, but I wish she didn't keep chickens. Or that Bean wasn't so excited about herding them.

Logan takes my arm and mutters in my ear. "C'mon, let's get out of here. I'll bring her a pint of gelato later." He raises his voice again. "See you, Rosa."

Muttering, she stalks back inside her own bungalow as the chickens fluff their feathers, cluck self-righteously at Bean, and resume pecking at the ground. But I'm sure at least one beady eye on each head stays on the retreating canine.

Back inside our house, I unhook the leash and lean against the kitchen counter, looking at my dog. "Bean, what am I going to do with you?"

Recognizing my disappointed tone, she collapses on the ground, her muzzle on top of her front paws and her eyes upturned to my face, expression mournful. When I don't relent, she whines and rolls onto her side, showing her belly. How can I stay upset with her when she looks so contrite?

I sit cross-legged next to her and stroke her super soft, fine fur. I don't know if it soothes her when I pet her, but it works for me. Like a lot of border collies, she's black along the top of her body, white on her legs and underside, and she has a streak of white around her muzzle and up her nose to the top of her head. The fur around her eyes is black, and the tip of her tail is white.

Logan grabs a reusable water bottle from the fridge, and as he shuts the door, a rumpled and worn piece of paper flutters out from under a Colorado-shaped magnet and falls beside me. While Logan twists the bottle open and drinks, I pick the paper up and absentmindedly scan the familiar faded handwritten items on my list.

Stevie's Bucket List
(To Do Before Age 30)

1. Change someone's life for the better.
2. Go skydiving.
3. Travel somewhere new.
4. Establish a healthy work-life balance.
5. Floss every night.
6. Organize my room and keep it clean.
7. Learn to do something new.
8. Learn to make gumbo.
9. Exercise every day.
10. Fall in love.

"She needs a hobby." Logan points the bottom of the bottle at Bean. "Something other than herding chickens."

Bean cocks her ear at that. She's an intelligent dog, but she can't possibly know the meaning of *hobby*. She must know the word *chicken*. I wouldn't be at all surprised by that.

"Like what?" I ask.

"I could take her jogging with me," he says.

I eye his trim, tanned legs, sun-bronzed face, and ever-present running shoes. "You don't jog, you sprint. You'd wear her out."

"She'd be fine. She's young and fit." He scratches his head. His black curls are thick and full when long, a little like a poodle's, so he keeps them cut pretty short. "Maybe there's a farm where you can pay for her to go herd something that actually needs herding. I've read about places like that."

"That's an idea. But it doesn't sound close by."

He groans. "You and driving. You should live in a city where you can take public transportation all the time."

"Like London. I've never been there."

"Pretty rainy for a Colorado girl. How about San Francisco?"

I think about it. "Too crowded."

He snorts. "But London's okay?"

Something I saw earlier plucks at my memory. I tug my phone out of the back pocket of my skinny jeans, where it lives most of the day, and tap on yesterday's email from Nextdoor. It usually contains things like alerts about crime in our Park Hill, Denver neighborhood, missing pets, items for sale, and community news. A posting I'd skimmed over had caught my eye.

"This. This is perfect." I push myself up off the floor and feel crumbs stuck on my palm. Ew. I wipe them off on my jeans and read the notice to Logan and Bean. She listens, head tilted, like she understands me.

"Join the Denver Disc Dogs club. We're looking for a few high-flying dogs and their enthusiastic humans to join our club. We'll help train your pup to catch frisbee discs and perform/compete with the club. Competitions are fun and affordable. All you need is a willingness to learn, an energetic, athletic dog, and an appropriate disc. Meet up with us on Wednesday nights at seven behind the Museum of Nature and Science in City Park."

An email address for someone named Emmy is listed if more information is needed. Bean wags her tail as I finish.

"See?" I say. "She likes this idea."

Logan shakes his head. "She likes the excitement in your voice."

"What's not to like? Bean's a good jumper, she catches treats easily, and I'll bet she'd love to train and mess around with the other dogs." And, to top it all off, she and I can walk to City Park. No driving required. "Maybe we'll go tomorrow night."

"It's worth checking out," Logan concedes.

Bean walks over and scratches the cabinet where I keep the container of her food.

"Dinner time already?" I ask her.

"She wouldn't let you forget, that's for sure," Logan says.

I pour Bean's kibble into her bowl and refresh her water. "What about us? I can whip up a salad with the leftover chicken."

"Shh," Logan puts a finger to his mouth, "they'll hear you." He glances around furtively.

"Who?"

"Rosa's hens." He grins. "If they know we're eating their kind in here, there could be an all-out revolt."

I laugh, and he pushes me gently toward the fridge.

"I'll make dinner. You can assist. After, all you've been hard at it all day."

I yawn. "Last night, too. But you worked all day, and I know all those facts and figures have taxed your brain." Logan's an accountant, or as I like to call him, a bean counter. Which is how Beanie got her name.

"Eh, today wasn't bad. And anyway, my salads are better. I put fruit in there, and those fried onion things, and nuts and stuff. I'm the salad king."

"Then what does that make me?" I ask. Bean wags her thin tail and looks from Logan to me.

Logan tosses me a fake withering look. "The salad wench, of course. Salad wench," he changes his voice into a command, "bring forth the lettuce and cucumbers and tomatoes from the icebox. I wish to look upon and chop all the slightly wilted produce forthwith." He grabs a chopping knife and waves it imperiously toward the fridge.

I curtsy to him. "Yes, my liege."

He grins. "I like it. Except I wish to be called My Lord and Salad Master."

It's my turn to scoff. "Don't push your luck."

As I walk to the refrigerator and slide my Things to Do Before I'm Thirty list back under the magnet, a familiar, uncomfortable feeling clutches at me as I recall the unwritten eleventh item.

Logan and I grew up together here in Park Hill. Back when we were six years old, we'd kissed and promised to get married someday. While on a break from college years ago, we'd had a few too many beers and renewed our vow. Then, three years ago at a mutual friend's boozy wedding, Logan had reminded me that we were both still single, and thirty was coming soon. I'd laughed it off then, but my thirtieth birthday is in August. Logan turned thirty in May.

We haven't talked about it again, but I know we both think about it.

He's the kindest, most thoughtful, most loyal guy on the planet. If I were a different girl, I would have jumped on him long ago. But I'm me, Stevie Watson, a sloppy, stubborn tomboy with a semi-obsessive love for graphic design and my border collie.

Logan's had plenty of girlfriends, but somehow, he always talks himself out of making a commitment to them. I've only dated a few men, and most of them annoyed the heck out of me.

So here we are in our shared kitchen, still single. We've got careers, friends, families, and an overly energetic dog. It's all good. Really good. I don't want to wreck what we have.

We're friends. Best friends. And housemates. Period.

But as I paw through the crisper drawer for edible vegetables, I feel restless. Life *is* good, but I think it's time—time to tackle the bucket list.

I won't ever check off unwritten item eleven, but I can accomplish number seven: *learn to do something new.*

I'll take Bean to the Denver Disc Dogs club.

It's new, and it's progress. And that's something.

Chapter Two

Logan

I knock on Stevie's partially open door before sticking my head into her room slash office.

"I'm headed out for a run . . ." My voice trails off as I glance around. My best friend and housemate isn't the cleanest or most organized at the best of times, but today might mark a new record of complete disarray.

Her bed's unmade. Books, dirty clothes, and used towels straggle across the floor. Her desk groans with half-drunk tea mugs, crumby plates, bound notebooks thrown open, and various Apple devices. And to top it all off, she's asleep on top of her keyboard. Her giant monitor shows a screen almost half-full of the letter E. Bean wags her tail at me from the bed.

"Stevie? You okay?" I ask.

One of her blue eyes pops open. She sits up slowly, and blinking in the late afternoon sun, squints at me.

"What? What time is it?" She sounds like an elderly frog.

I check my watch. "Six."

She peers at the screen and leans back in her chair. She's still wearing the same clothes as yesterday.

"Late night last night?" I ask.

"Yeah." She rubs her face. "I got started on a new project."

I want to laugh at the keyboard key marks imprinted on her cheek, but instead I nod, understanding the subtext. New projects envelop Stevie like a comfy blanket, soft couch, and satisfying Netflix binge might for a normal person.

After our salads last night, we'd made a pint-sized chocolate-caramel gelato peace offering for Rosa and taken Bean for a quick after-dinner stroll. Then, I'd gone to bed. The workday comes early in the accounting world.

Stevie's room was quiet this morning, so without peeking in, I'd let Bean out to use the yard, escorted her back in, and left for work. Stevie had probably worked feverishly until she sacked out on her desk.

She stands, stretches, shakes her head of wavy dark blonde hair, and finally looks more alert. "I need to grab something to eat so I can get Bean over to City Park by seven."

"I can meet you there after my run," I say.

She brightens. "Lovely! It'll be fun. I decided it will count as number seven on my list. C'mon Bean, dinner time."

The collie jumps up, tail swishing wildly.

I follow them into the kitchen. "Your list?"

She sticks a thumb out at the paper on the refrigerator. "My thirtieth birthday bucket list. I'm finally going to start on it."

My muscles tense. The list has been there for so long, constantly falling off the fridge door, that I'd almost forgotten about it. It's like old wallpaper or a piece of neglected furniture. Invisible. What's driving Stevie to go after it now?

"Right," I say. "Sounds good. See you at the park."

When I grab my AirPods and phone out of my room, it's impossible not to notice how different my space is from hers. My bed is made, clothes hang neatly in my closet, my bathroom is spotless, and not an item is out of place. As an accountant, I thrive on order.

Which has sometimes caused conflicts with the creative down the hall.

I breathe deeply as I start my run, partly to fill my lungs and prepare them for the exertion, partly to release the pent-up frustration with Stevie that seems to grow with every passing year.

I don't care that she's not a great housekeeper, that she leaves her stuff lying around in mismatched piles, that I'll sometimes find her asleep in a patio chair or in the middle of the living room floor if that's where she'd been inspired to work the night before. All of that stuff makes her fascinating to me. What I mind is that I'm thirty now, and she's close enough to thirty to touch it, we're approaching thirty, and she hasn't said a word about our agreement.

My feet pound the ground a little harder than they should and sweat breaks out on my forehead. It's a lot warmer today than yesterday. No clouds cover the sun, and for the first part of my run, I'm on asphalt, passing brick and stucco homes built sometime in the first half of the twentieth century. There are also a growing number of modern homes and a handful of actual McMansions on too-small lots.

The crown jewel of this area, though, is City Park, which is where I'm headed now. The Denver Museum of Nature and Science sits at the eastern end of the park, the Denver Zoo runs along the north side, and there's a lake and pavilion in the middle, along with several playgrounds and plenty of green space for picnicking or lolling.

I rarely loll.

As I run, I wonder what it means that Stevie's finally tackling her bucket list. She's ignored that thing for so long, I'd thought about hiding it to see if she'd notice. She's always been a procrastinator, and thirty is around the corner, now.

Some of the items should be doable, like trying something new and flossing, but others aren't so easy to accomplish. I think about her item number ten as I speed across Colorado Boulevard to beat the pedestrian signal count down. *Fall in love.*

Stevie hasn't even dated anyone since Enrique last year. He was a nice guy, but when they'd broken up, she'd said he'd texted and called too much. Most women would be happy about that. Not her.

I run a hand through my hair. Stevie drives me up a wall. Many walls. I try not to think too hard about why.

But a memory swims to me of a friend's wedding up in Vail that we went to a few years ago, the last time I brought up the bargain our six-year-old selves had made.

We'd been dancing with friends and decided to take a break outside. The sun was setting over the mountains, and the view was spectacular. I'd had one too many cocktails from the open bar, and Stevie looked drop-dead gorgeous. Tendrils of her hair escaped from the loose knot she'd twisted it into, and she wore one of her two dresses, the low-cut black one, and a rare pair of high heels that I don't think I've seen since. She was pink faced with champagne and laughing, and I'd touched her soft cheek without thinking.

"So, are we still going to do it?" I asked her.

Her forehead wrinkled, but she giggled. "Do what?"

"Get married."

Her smile faded, and she turned away to look at the peaks as the sun tipped behind them. "Sure. Of course we will. We agreed, right?"

My heart pumped hard in my chest. "Okay, let's shake on it. If we're still single by the time we're thirty, we'll get together."

She turned toward me, her face pale. "Thirty?"

"We need a deadline," I joked, "or we'll never make a decision." I stuck out my hand, and, hesitatingly, she shook it.

That would have been the perfect time for a kiss to seal the deal . . . but I'd left it at that, and I haven't mentioned it since. I'd met Felicia soon after anyway, and we'd dated until six months ago. She was an attorney, a great girl and a lot of fun, and she'd talked about moving in together.

But I couldn't pull the trigger. Moving in with Felicia would have meant moving out of the house that Stevie and I had shared since graduating from college. Probably unsurprisingly, Felicia had broken up with me a few weeks later.

Stevie and I have a good thing going. I don't want to mess with it. But I feel a clock ticking ominously somewhere inside me, telling me time is running out. Not for marriage or family or anything like that. The time until she turns thirty.

I've known since I was six years old that I'd marry Stevie Watson, but we don't seem any closer to taking any action on our vow than when we were kids. I've been waiting for her to show me she's ready.

Is it time to make my feelings for her clear?

Or should I keep waiting?

Chapter Three

Stevie

City Park is usually well loved on nice summer days. Even on nice winter days. Today's no different.

As Bean and I cross over Colorado Boulevard to the museum and then walk around it, we pass runners, walkers, bikers, families with little kids, skateboarders, and even a cat on a leash.

Bean trots beside me, ears and tail up, eyes bright. She peers warily at the pack of metallic wolf statues spread outside of the museum entrance, while I peer inside the glass doors at the two-story reconstructed T-rex skeleton in the lobby. The museum is closed for the day, but the dinosaur bones are visible through the windows and bathed in late afternoon light. Actually, I'm not even sure they're real bones. I think it's a model. Either way, I love that I can casually spot a T-rex while walking to the local park from our home.

Bean sniffs a tree for a sec, then hurries back to my side. She's a great walker—not one of those pee-on-every-blade-of-grass type dogs. She seems to intuitively know when a walk is for her, meaning a stroll where she can luxuriate in soaking up every rich scent and interesting sight versus when it's for me, like for exercise, or when we need to be somewhere.

Like now. I check my watch; we've got five minutes to find the group.

On the other side of the museum, the park spreads out. There's Ferril Lake in the center of the park, a great view of the downtown skyline in the distance, and beyond that, the foothills of the Rocky Mountains. I have to pause for a second to admire. The buildings downtown are silhouettes, but I can make out the snow frosting the upper peaks of the mountains.

Mmm. Frosting.

I'd only had time for a protein bar and a banana, so no wonder I'm hungry.

Shading my eyes from the sun, I spot a group of dogs and humans in a wide stretch of grass between the museum and the lake. People walk and run along the trails around the water, but the field where this group gathers is fairly empty.

"C'mon, Bean. There they are."

We speed walk over, and when we reach the group, stop to watch. The field is marked into a rectangle by long ropes tied to four orange cones at each corner. Six humans stand at one of the narrow ends of the rectangle and throw flexible discs short distances for their dogs to chase and catch. As we watch, a border collie that looks a lot like Bean leaps into the air to catch the disc thrown for her, while a brown and white shepherd-looking dog runs after his and misses. Bean pays close attention beside me.

A petite woman splits off from the group and comes our way. She has long, glossy brown hair, trim legs that are perfectly showcased in cut-off denim shorts, and she's wearing a T-shirt with a logo on it for a company called Hyperflite. Sunglasses and a visor cover her face, but I can tell at a glance she's very pretty. She greets me with a smile.

"Hi, are you here for the Denver Disc Dogs club?"

I nod and wave. "I'm Stevie, and this is Bean. I saw your posting in Nextdoor."

"Oh, great! I'm glad those things work. It's hard to tell sometimes, you know? I'm Emmy, the captain of the club. My dog Meadow is a border collie, too. Jude is warming her up for me." She points to the dog I saw flying across the field a minute ago. She's bringing a frisbee back to a cute Latino guy. He's lean and muscular, with messy black hair and wearing long camouflage shorts and flip flops.

"Has Bean ever played with a disc before?" Emmy asks.

"No. But I think she'll like it." I laugh. "She loves chasing things—like my neighbor's chickens—and she has plenty of energy to burn."

Emmy grins. "Got it. Before we started the club, Meadow almost got me kicked out of my apartment. She was so wild." She's about to say something else, I think, when her eyes fix on something behind me.

It's Logan. He slows from a jog to a walk, his tan skin glowing in the sun. As I turn back to Emmy, I notice she can't quite tear her gaze away from him. I don't blame her. Even soaked in sweat, he's a handsome guy. I introduce him to her as my best friend and housemate.

"It's so nice to meet you both," Emmy says with a sweet smile. "Come on over, and we'll get started with some drills. You can watch for a while, and then I'll show you a few ways to get started with Bean's training. Did you happen to bring a disc?"

I shake my head. "No, sorry. I saw the post yesterday."

"No problem. You can borrow one of mine this week to try out. If Bean likes it, I'll give you a list of good brands. She won't know what to do with the disc at first, of course, but I'll bet with a week or two of training at home, she'll be ready to fly."

We follow Emmy over to the group, and she makes some quick introductions. Bean wags her tail and sniffs at the other dogs, who pant and sniff her back. Emmy speaks to the group.

"Why don't we do a little demo to get things started? Show Stevie, Logan, and Bean what they can look forward to."

Logan and I step back as the rest of the group stands at a rope line. Then, one by one, they throw their discs toward the far end of the rectangle. The dogs tear off after them, some catching the disc as it comes down, and some missing it. Meadow and one other dog are able to leap up to catch the discs in midair. They immediately bring them back to their humans, and stand, staring at them, tails wagging, until the disc is thrown again. Emmy turns music on through a portable speaker, and the demo starts to feel more like a performance than a training. Bean whines, probably jealous that the other dogs run free.

The humans throw the discs in a choreographed way, and most of the dogs wait, and watch carefully for their time to run. A few seem distracted, wandering away to sniff something in the grass or leaving the rectangle all together, forcing their humans to chase them.

After a couple of minutes of the throwing and catching, Emmy hands her disc to Jude. "So that was throw and catch, one fun disc event, and this is another. It's called freestyle."

Jude drops three discs at his feet and holds one more out with a straight arm for Meadow to jump up and grab. She gives it back to him, he lunges, and she runs between his legs a few times. He twists one way, and she runs the other, and he tosses the frisbee for her to leap and catch, then he lunges again, leans forward to pick up another disc and she runs up his outstretched back leg and along his spine to jump and grab it when he tosses it into the air in front of her.

Logan and I clap as Emmy turns the music off and the group rewards the dogs with treats. Bean yips a few times, looking more than ready to get started.

Emmy smiles. "That was a taste of what you and Bean can do if you join. And if you both like it, of course."

"That was incredible," I say to Jude. "How long did it take for her to learn that?"

"Thanks." He smiles and fluffs Meadow's fur. "A few years. I was the slow one. Meadow is Emmy's dog, but we've been friends for a while, so I work with her, too."

"Some of us have been training for longer than others," Emmy says, "but within a few weeks, a dog is usually able to start catching short throws, and with consistency, the rest comes."

She speaks to the group again. "Why don't you guys work on your distance throws, and I'll help Stevie, Logan, and Bean get started with a few activities."

Everyone lines up at the end of the marked-out rectangle and starts throwing their discs again. The dogs run joyfully after them. It's kind of heartwarming to see.

Emmy takes us a little way away. "Can I take Bean's leash for a bit?" I hand it to her, and Emmy holds out a disc for Bean to sniff. Then she lays it upside down on the ground in front of her and fishes a treat out of her pocket to put in it.

"So, the first thing you can and should do is to feed Bean in the disc," she says. "Let her eat out of it. After a week or so of that, you can put treats in it, like this, and start moving it back and forth in front of her nose. Make sure she's paying attention. Maybe even toss it a couple of feet. Pretty soon, she'll decide that a frisbee is something she likes."

I laugh and point at my dog, who's licking Emmy's disc. "I think she's already decided that."

The captain claps for her. "That was fast." She tilts her head and pulls her hair over her shoulder. "Let's try a little experiment." She picks up the disc and holds it front of Bean's face, then moves it back and forth. Bean's nose follows it. "What do you think, Bean, do you want to chase it?"

Emmy digs another treat out of her shorts. As she does, I catch Logan glancing down at her legs. Again, can't blame him. She's lovely. She puts the treat in the upside-down disc and shows it to Bean, who stares at it, wagging her tail.

"Go get it, girl!" Emmy skims the frisbee a few feet along the ground. Bean runs after it and gobbles up the treat. Then she licks the disc and nudges it forward a couple of times, as if that might make another treat magically appear.

We laugh, and Emmy rewards Bean with another treat from her pocket. "I think she'll pick this up quickly. Since she seems food motivated, be sure to have lots of treats on hand, or at least handfuls of kibble."

"I will." I pick up the disc, toss it up a foot, and catch it. Bean barks, and Logan nudges me.

"I think she wants you to throw it again."

My dog stands, her head tilted to the side, eyes on the disc. I sling it. I can't say it's a great throw, but sure enough, Bean tears after it.

"Wow," Emmy says. "She's a smart girl."

I beam with pride. "I've always thought so."

Bean sniffs all around the disc when it lands, even using her nose to flip it over onto the other side, but she doesn't bring it back. Not that I expected her to the first time.

Emmy watches her. "You might be able to shorten the introduction stuff. I'd feed her in the disc for a few days and maybe play around in the backyard or whatever with a treat in the disc. Ask her to pick it up when you throw it and be sure to reward her if she does."

Bean barks at the disc, obviously wanting it to fly again. Logan walks over to retrieve it.

"I'm going to go work with Meadow for a while. You guys are welcome to join us and keep throwing for Bean." Emmy winks. "You never know, she might be catching it before the end of the hour."

"Thanks for the tips," I say. "I'll work with her this week."

"We're here every Wednesday at seven, and a lot of times we head over to Station 26 for beers afterward. The dogs come with us. We aren't going this week, but we probably will next Wednesday."

"Great, sounds fun," I say. Emmy walks away as Logan returns. He watches her go.

"Nice woman," I say.

"Yeah," Logan's eyes flick to me.

"Pretty, too." I quirk a brow.

He elbows me. "Think so? Are you going to ask her out?"

I roll my eyes. "No, but maybe you should. You two would make a hot couple."

He pauses for a second to look at me, then shakes his head and walks on.

What did I say? I was teasing him. Sometimes I wonder if I know Logan as well as I think I do.

That thought rolls around like a marble in the back of my head while we watch the others, and for a while after, too.

Chapter Four

Logan

That night, I shower, eat a sandwich, and sit down to play a round of *Redemption* with my buddy, Noah. We're going after a pair of alien marauders bent on human destruction. The aliens look like humans, so there's always a risk of shooting perfectly normal humans and getting life points taken away ourselves, but Noah and I have been watching these two for a while.

I'm about to outline my plan of attack with Noah through my headset, when Stevie wanders into the living room flossing her teeth. Bean looks up at her from the couch beside me, and I stop mid-sentence.

"Be right back," I say to Noah.

I can hear him grouse, but I flip the headset to mute. "You're flossing."

Stevie nods absently. "Good dental hygiene is very important."

I eye her. She's wearing a pair of my old sweatpants and a cropped tank top with no bra. She's never worn a bra in the house, so long as other people weren't around. I know she doesn't think anything of it, because she thinks of me like a brother. But it drives this brother nuts.

I have to make a heroic effort to keep my eyes off her perfectly formed chest. I would never want to make her as uncomfortable as she unintentionally makes me.

I drag my eyes back to the television screen in an effort to look anywhere but at her. Noah's and my avatars are standing around watching the alley the aliens slipped down.

"Number five," I say.

She cocks her head with a questioning glance.

"On your bucket list."

"Yeah. I thought it was about time I tackled a few of those."

I grit my teeth grimly. I was right.

I turn back to the game, but I'm distracted now. What does this mean? Does she remember the unwritten item number eleven?

Of course she does. Stevie might be the flighty artsy type, but she has an excellent memory. And who could forget their first—and only—kiss with a best friend?

I remember it perfectly well myself. Stevie and I had been playing on the playset behind her house. Our parents were lucky; we could always be found in her backyard or mine. Stevie's mom, Carol, was already divorced. She worked full time as a receptionist back then. My dad worked in sales at an oil company, and Mom was and is a high school math teacher, so she'd keep an eye on both of us in the afternoons after school. In exchange, Carol would watch me and my brother Dylan on the weekends so our folks could run errands without dragging us with them or go out for dinner somewhere other than McDonalds. Carol hadn't met Lamar, her husband and Stevie's stepdad, yet.

Dylan, who must have been four at the time, had been sitting in the grass likely eating bugs or dirt or something equally gross, while Stevie and I swung on the swings. We'd all recently finished our Fudgsicles, and Stevie's pale face was covered in drying chocolate ice cream. Mine too, probably.

I can't remember what she'd been wearing but probably short shorts and a T-shirt. That's what she's pretty much always worn except for a brief stint in middle school when she went through a really girly phase and wore tiny skirts and cropped T-shirts. I hadn't minded.

"Are you going to get married when you grow up?" Stevie had suddenly asked.

I'd pumped my legs harder, trying to go higher and faster than she was. She always seemed to get her swing a little higher and a little faster than mine, no matter how hard I worked. "I dunno. I guess."

"My mom wants to get married again."

"How . . . do you . . . know?" I was out of breath from the pumping.

"I heard her talking to my auntie on the phone." She didn't say anything else for a minute.

"Who are you going to marry?" I ask.

"You, silly," she answered.

I slowed down at that, letting the swing go forward and backward but without pumping. By the time my swing stood still, Stevie had been stopped for a while. She stood next to her swing, hanging on to one chain, her wavy golden hair in a long tangle down her back.

Reaching down, she pulled up a blade of grass and stepped in front of me. "Hold out your hand."

I did, and she wrapped the grass around my pointer finger. Hey, we were six.

"Will you marry me, Logan Stephens?"

I looked into her gray blue eyes, or at least I liked to think I did, and said, "Yep."

And she'd kissed me. Her lips tasted like chocolate.

And that was it. We'd talked about the vow, as I like to think of it, a few times over the years, usually when drunk and a little bummed that we were both still single, but we'd never kissed again, and we hadn't really had a serious discussion about the possibility.

As I blow away one of the aliens, narrowly missing Noah's avatar, which makes him yell in my ear, I wonder, why is that? Why haven't we talked about getting together? Or freaking gotten together already? We live in the same house, after all, it wouldn't be hard. It would be a matter of a nice bottle of wine, some mood music, and some talking, hopefully followed by a lot of kissing.

I haven't ever brought it up, because I've always gotten the sense it needed to be her decision. I'd been her choice at age six; was I still at age thirty? I've never admitted this to anyone, but if she'd come to me at any time over the last few years and said she was ready to get romantically involved, I'd have said yes in a flash.

But she hadn't.

So . . . now what? Do I let her work her list and hope she gets to number eleven? Do I playfully remind her of our agreement again? Or do I do the mature thing and tell her how I feel about her?

The thought of that makes my muscles tense up and my stomach sour. Telling her that could change everything between us. It could make our relationship incredibly . . . awkward.

Stevie and I have something special, after all. We've been friends since childhood and housemates since college. We've always had each other's backs and never had a serious fight.

But the last year or so she'd grown a little more distant, like she felt the big 3-0 deadline bearing down on us as much as I did.

And now it's almost here.

I have to do something to persuade her that what we have is not only worth preserving but worth deepening into something new.

I have to show her I love her like more than a friend. Like a man loves a woman.

But how?

Chapter Five

Stevie

The morning after the disc dogs club, I wake up late and dress in a hurry. Luckily, it doesn't take me very long.

I own five pairs of skinny jeans for fall, five pairs of shorts for summer, a collection of T-shirts and hoodies, and a smattering of bead bracelets and some hoop and dangly earrings. Plus, two dresses and a couple of fancier tops for occasions that call for them. What can I say? I work from home. And I have enough decisions in my life. What I wear is not one I'm interested in making every day.

I've read that the contents of my closet could be called a capsule wardrobe. I call it easy. And I'm all for easy.

Because of my nocturnal work habits, Logan feeds and lets Bean out early before he heads to work downtown. Now, she waits for me by the front door, tail wagging, as I jam my feet into shoes and grab her leash. She knows where we're going as well as I do. It's Thursday morning, after all.

I duck and Bean leaps into my mother's black Lexus SUV and we both kiss her cheek. She greets my dog with a scratch on the chest and a gentle shove into the backseat and me with a smile and a soft palm against my cheek.

"Morning, Stevie Sunshine."

She's always greeted me this way, no matter what was going on in our lives: divorce (her), uncontrolled moodiness (me, mainly in middle and high school), almost dropping out of high school (me, only didn't because Logan did most of my math homework for me), being laid off (her), actually dropping out of college (me), and remarrying a great guy, Lamar (her).

She eyes me as she backs out of my driveway. "Did you get enough sleep last night? You look tired."

I flip down the visor and check out my face in the mirror. She's right. "Not really. I got to working on a project. But I'll survive."

She sighs. "You really should get more sleep, love. Before you know it, you'll get married, have babies, and then you'll go through menopause. And most of those things lead to a lack of sleep."

"To do two out of three of those things, I have to meet someone first," I counter.

Mom eyes me but doesn't say anything. She always gets cagey when I talk about never meeting the right guy. I have no idea why.

She's fashionably dressed as usual in black slacks, heels, a baby pink silk shell, and a matching summer cardigan. Her dark blonde, shoulder-length, wavy hair is styled, and her makeup is on point, but she couldn't quite cover up the smudges of fatigue under her eyes. "Bad night?"

She groans. "I had hot flashes half the time and spent the rest having to pee."

I frown. And now she's taking time out of her busy day to drive me to my stepsister Tamara's house thanks to my pathological hatred of driving.

"But I love getting to see you," Mom adds sweetly. I swear the woman can read my mind.

I touch her arm. "You, too. Thanks for the ride."

After being laid off from a receptionist job at a commercial real estate office, Mom got her real estate license. Now, she's really busy with tons of referrals, and yet, her schedule is fairly flexible. Driving me places once in a while, like to Tamara's house on Thursday mornings to babysit, is one way we carve out some time to see each other in her crazy week.

Tamara, her husband Dean, and their daughter Jasmine live in Montclair, a neighborhood about ten minutes south of Park Hill, where Logan, Mom, Lamar, and I live. Mom helped Tamara and Dean buy their home during a rare downturn in the Denver housing market. They're both public school teachers, so money is pretty tight. Logan and I rent our house.

A whine from Bean draws my attention. She's staring out the side window at a couple of squirrels chasing each other around in someone's front yard.

Bean is the gentlest creature on earth, I swear, but she absolutely cannot resist the urge to chase and herd. Whenever there are more than two creatures of the same species, including small humans, she wants to push them together, keep them together, and make sure they're safe. If only the creatures knew that was her intent.

"Did you finish that logo you were working on?" Mom asks.

I nod. "It turned out pretty well. Choppy liked it." Mom had referred Choppy to me, so I was extra invested in making sure he was happy. "How was your day yesterday?"

"Long, but good. Some clients that had been looking for a home for months finally closed, so that was a relief."

We chat about the clients she'll see today, and after a few minutes I ask, "Mom, do you think Lamar would show me how to make gumbo this weekend?"

She blinks with surprise. "I'm sure he would. But . . . why?"

I play with the peeling tread of my Converse sneaker. Time for a new pair soon. With my limited footwear, I wear them out pretty quickly. "I've been wanting to learn for a while."

"I know. I mean, why now?"

Mom has probably seen the bucket list on our fridge hundreds of times. The items on there are no secret.

As for item number five, Lamar offered to show me how to make his family's top-secret gumbo recipe years ago. He's from south Louisiana, and his grandmother passed it down to him on the condition that he'd swear to keep it in the family. That he considers me family, even though we aren't blood, is an honor.

I consider how to answer my mother's question. "Well, I'm not getting any younger."

She sighs. "Ain't that the truth."

"And I want to check a few things off the thirtieth birthday bucket list."

Her hands tighten slightly on the wheel. "What else have you done?"

"Logan and I took Bean to the Denver Disc Dogs club last night, so that's something new. Oh! And I flossed."

"Astonishing!" Mom says with an ironic eyebrow raise. "No, that's really great, Stevie. I'm glad you're going to accomplish some things you've wanted to do for a long time."

She gets that thoughtful look on her face again as she pulls into the driveway of my sister's one-story ranch home and turns the car off.

"Coming in?" I ask.

"I thought I would," she reaches for her purse down by my feet. I hand it to her. "I have a little time before my next showing."

Bean explodes with joy in the backseat, whining and probably scratching the leather seats. I hurry to let her out. She leaps to the ground and rockets to the front door, barking.

Jazzy throws the door open and Bean almost knocks my niece on her butt as they greet each other. Their excitement to see each other is the sweetest moment of my week. Jazzy is a tornado of color, her latest clothing trend. She wears hot pink high-top shoes, lemon yellow shorts, a turquoise shirt, and her big floof of light brown curly hair is secured in a topknot by a rainbow-colored hair band. The hues all look beautiful against her copper brown skin. She has golden eyes like her mother and is tall for her age like her dad.

Dog and girl run straight through to the backyard to play, while my mother and I stop in the cozy living room to greet Tamara and Dean.

My sister is three years older than me and drop-dead gorgeous. She has shoulder-length dark brown hair that she usually wears in a smooth style, large, honey-tinged brown eyes, dark brown skin with a smattering of light freckles, and a perfect figure. Dean, who's five years older than Tamara, has graying dark hair and an olive complexion, and he's equally as fit.

"Where are you guys headed today?" I ask after we hug and say hello. "You look like you're getting ready for an expedition to the Amazon." They're wearing workout clothes with rain jackets and waterproof sandals. A hiking backpack and two large plastic water bottles sit on the counter in the kitchen.

"Up to Clear Creek to do some kayaking," Dean says.

"You're entirely too healthy." I pause, thinking. "I actually can't remember the last time I exercised."

Tamara shakes her head ruefully. "You're welcome to come on Adventure Thursday any time, you know."

I lift my hands in surrender and shake my head. "Bringing me along might end up being more of an adventure than you bargained for."

Adventure Thursday is a tradition Tamara and Dean started when they first got married. As teachers, they have summers off except for tutoring and a few part-time hustles they do to make extra money. So, they'd made a commitment to do something new and fun every Thursday. The Rocky Mountains are chock full of outdoorsy challenges like hiking, rock climbing, rafting, parachuting off peaks, hot air ballooning . . . you name it, and we have it here. And over the years, Tamara and Dean had tried it all. For the last couple of summers, Mom, Lamar, or I had babysat Jazzy so that they could go.

Speak of the devil, my niece busts in from the backyard. "Aunt Stevie, guess what? Bean learned a new trick."

Tamara clucks at her daughter. "Inside voice, please, Jasmine."

Jazzy scowls. She came up with her own nickname and gets grumpy when anyone doesn't use it, including her parents. My mother scoops her granddaughter up in her arms and hugs her. Technically, Jazzy is her step-granddaughter, but Mom never calls her that.

"How are you, little miss?" Mom asks, kissing her cheek and twirling her around.

"Good, Gramma, but wait, I have to show you Bean's trick —" She squirms to be put back down.

"Okay, Jazzy! Hang on, I'm talking with your parents right now. I'll be right there. How was the water park yesterday?" Mom asks Tam.

My sister groans. "So crowded. But Jazzy had fun. Right Jazz?"

"Yes, but—" Jazzy points to the back door.

Dean winks at Mom and me. "Wore her out, too. She took a two-hour nap when we got home."

Mom's eyes go wide. "Two hours? Our girl took a two-hour nap?"

Tamara and Dean nod with satisfaction and high five each other.

Jazzy's been trying to speak, but the adults keep interrupting her. Finally, she grabs the hem of my shorts.

I bend down on one knee so she can hear me. "What's Bean's trick, Jazz?"

She throws her hands up dramatically. "*That's* what I've been trying to *tell* you. She learned to dig under the fence!"

I stand. "What?"

"Yeah, she went that way." She points to the side fence.

Dean steps to the back door and looks out. "She's not here."

"Do you have any chicken in the house?" I ask.

Tamara nods. "Leftover kabobs from last night."

"Can I grab a piece or two?" I ask.

"I'll get them," Mom says.

"Okay next question," I ask. "Do you have any chickens as neighbors?"

"What?" Tamara's brow wrinkles.

"Backyard chicken coops?"

"Oh." She thinks about it. "Dean, doesn't someone keep chickens around the corner on 8th?"

He nods. "About halfway down the block. Think that's where she's headed?"

"I have a bad feeling," I say.

Mom hurries out of the kitchen with the cooked variety of chicken wrapped in a paper towel. "Want help?"

"No, but can you stay here with Jazzy, please? I'll be right back. You two have fun!" I say to Tamara and Dean.

I rush out the door, calling for Bean. Jazzy complains to her parents that she wants to help find Bean too, but frankly a six-year-old is more hazard than help when you're trying to locate something quickly.

I jog in the direction Jazzy pointed and Dean indicated, ears peeled for Bean's excited bark. Sure enough, I hear her. As I close in on her location, I note the familiar squawks of a flock of frightened fowl. An elderly female voice croaks, "Get out of my yard, beast!"

I dart inside the chain-link fence to find a white-haired woman in a pistachio green bathrobe brandishing the business end of a broom at Bean who seems completely oblivious of the threat. My dog barks and runs at the chickens, darting in toward the flock here and there to prevent any of them from making a great escape. Even though they aren't really trying to.

"Bean, come here!" I hold out the cooked chicken. "Look, girl, chicken. Your favorite!"

Bean looks torn. She barks at a terrified hen that was trying to sneak toward the coop, but then her black nose twitches my way. For a moment, it looks like the live chickens will win out over the edible version. Then, she gives up and trots over to me to accept her prize. I seize her collar.

"I'm so sorry—" I start to say to the woman, but when I meet her eyes, she looks scandalized. "Don't feed that horrible dog chicken in front of my flock!"

I stammer. "I, uh, I mean, I was trying to get her—"

"Savage! Brute!" The woman yells at Bean and me. "Get out of my yard, both of you!" She twists the broom around and thrusts the handle end my way like a sword or javelin. I pull Bean out of her reach.

"Yes, ma'am, we're leaving." As my border collie chows down on the rest of the meat, I hustle her out of the yard, a hand on her collar. She casts a last, sorry look back at the flustered hens and the indignant woman, but then walks calmly by my side back to Tamara and Dean's house.

This is getting out of hand. Bean needs a distraction from her fowl obsession. If she doesn't take to the disc chasing, we'll have to find something else. Because this kind of behavior can't continue.

Either Bean will end up in animal jail, or a feathered friend will end up in hen heaven. And I'm determined not to see either of those things happen.

Chapter Six

Logan

I love every run I take, always have, but for various reasons some are better than others. This one, on a regular Wednesday after-noon, is special because the weather's great, and I get to hear the monkeys.

Let me be clear: monkeys are not indigenous to Denver, Colorado.

But they do hang out at the Denver Zoo, which backs up to City Park. So, sometimes, as I run past the perimeter wall, I hear them calling to each other with their high-pitched screeches and lower howls. It's pretty cool.

Then, within minutes, I spot the graylag goose couple. These birds are large and—you guessed it—gray, with creamy white tail feathers, a garish orange beak, and pink legs. Graylags normally live in Europe, but this pair obviously got lost somewhere around Iceland and now summer at Duck Lake, a pond in the park that borders the zoo side. I keep an eye out for them on my runs.

Why do I watch for geese while running? Okay, I'll admit it, I love birds. Amateur ornithology is my jam, a hobby I learned from my dad. On summer evenings when I was growing up, we'd go out around the neighborhood with binoculars and a bird book and spot different species like flickers, woodpeckers, nuthatches, and hummingbirds. Stevie sometimes came with us.

It's not the hippest hobby a thirty-year-old guy can have, but what can I say. I like it. And Stevie thinks it's cool, so there's that.

Anyway, the graylags paddle around on the lake, along with various diving ducks like widgeons, scaups, dabblers, and the scads of Canada geese that always seem to be around. I slow to a walk and watch the geese and ducks for a minute as they plunge headfirst into the water in search of food.

Life isn't easy for any animal on this planet, and I've always admired birds' ability to look casually unperturbed while doing their best to survive the effects of us humans, plus Mother Nature.

I check my watch. Time to meet Stevie and Bean at the club meeting. I jog that way, and zero in on them immediately. I'd never say this out loud, but I have a weird internal homing device when it comes to Stevie.

Ever since we were kids, I've always known when she was around. Like, I could tell if she was in my backyard before she knocked. Or if she rolled her bike out of the garage before she had a chance to text me to go somewhere with her. One time, during our senior year at Denver East High School, which happens to sit on the opposite side of City Park from the zoo, I'd asked a friend of Stevie's if she'd seen her. She said she thought Stevie had gone home. But I knew she was there. I felt her. And more than that, I had the feeling she was upset.

Feeling like a weirdo, but convinced I was right, I'd lurked outside the girl's bathroom. Sure enough, Stevie had come out a couple of minutes later, her eye makeup streaked under her eyes and clutching a wad of tissues. Her jerk boyfriend had broken up with her after sixth period, and she'd spent the rest of the afternoon crying in a stall.

Instead of a Spidey-sense, I have a Stevie-sense.

Now, she's talking to Emmy and Jude while Bean sits and watches the other dogs run after their discs.

Stevie greets me with a smile. "I was about to show them what Bean has learned."

"It's pretty amazing," I tell the others.

"Let's see what you and Bean got," Jude says to Stevie with a smile. I study him for a second. He's a good-looking dude, fit with a lot of thick dark hair. He's shorter than me, but only by a few inches.

Stevie pulls a peanut butter packet out of her pocket, tears it open and lets Bean sniff it, then she rubs a bit of butter on the edge of the disc. "I came up with this idea to get Bean interested in the disc even when it wasn't mealtime. It worked pretty well."

She holds the disc in front of Bean's nose, and when she's sufficiently focused, spins it about six feet away. Bean runs after it and licks the peanut butter off.

"Pick it up, Beanie," Stevie says. "Pick it up!"

After a second, Bean does.

"Okay, come back!" Stevie says. When Bean doesn't obey, Stevie gently tugs on the long lead she'd bought this week on Emmy's advice, and Bean trots back, looking proud.

Jude claps and Emmy smiles brightly. "That's amazing progress for one week."

Stevie rubs Bean's head. "I think she really enjoys it."

"She's ready for training, phase two," Jude says.

"What's phase two?" Stevie tilts her head and pushes her hair out of her face where it fell when she leaned over to pet Bean. I wish I wasn't so aware of her little movements like that.

"More of what you're already doing. Keep throwing the disc for her with the lead on," he says. "Start short and then throw it a little farther each time. While you're at it, you can work on your throw."

Stevie wrinkles her nose. "Am I that bad?"

Jude shakes his head and answers quickly. "No, not at all."

Emmy raises an eyebrow as Stevie and I smirk at the obvious lie.

"Everyone can use some work on throws," he clarifies. "I'll give you a few pointers now, if you want."

Stevie smiles. "Thanks, Jude. Sounds great."

Emmy glances at me as they walk off. "Want to help me work out with Meadow?" She leads me over to the group where her dog sits unleashed, calmly watching the other dogs run around.

"I can't believe how well trained she is," I say.

Emmy snatches an errant disc rolling toward us. She spins it smoothly back to the person, who yells thanks and immediately throws it for their dog. I think that pair was here last week, but I'm not sure.

"Meadow is like a short human with four legs and a fur coat," she says as she calls her over. "I've never really had to reward her with treats or food; she seems to know what I'm asking for and does it." She smiles at me. "Although, I *do* give her treats, of course. I mean, what kind of life would it be for a dog without treats?"

At the barest hint of a whistle, Meadow hustles over to her mistress. Emmy grabs a disc out of her backpack. "Ready to work, girl?"

The border collie wags her tail, her eyes fixed on the disc. Emmy steps up to the rope line, turns so her body is sideways and spins the disc, a smooth gesture that sends it flying straight and true and parallel to the ground. Meadow launches herself after it.

The dog doesn't have to leap to catch the frisbee; she collects it easily in her mouth at the end of its flight and runs back to offer it to Emmy.

"Wow. Clearly pros," I say.

"We've been doing this for years but thank you. I'm proud of her. Do you want to throw a few for her?" Emmy asks.

"Yeah, definitely. Although my throw won't look like yours."

She hands me the disc. "It doesn't have to. The dogs should

get used to all kinds of throws and catches, and it's important for them to practice them in training."

"Good thing," I joke, "because this might end up in the lake."

Emmy rubs Meadow's head and tilts her own at me. "Luckily for you, she's a good swimmer, too."

I take the disc. As I weigh it in my hand, prepared to not humiliate myself, I glance over at Stevie and Bean.

Jude stands close behind her, his dark head close to her blonde one, his arm wrapped around her, their hands together on the disc. Slowly, their hands and arms extend. My eyes narrow and my muscles tense.

Cool it, Logan. He's showing her how to improve her throw, like he said. I force my eyes back to the waiting Meadow, and then I curl my forearm and spin it. Too hard.

The frisbee goes straight for a second, and then curls right, almost skimming the back of a running dog down to the right. Meadow does her best to catch the disc I threw, but she has to dodge the dog, which destroys her timing. The frisbee lands with a hard thud.

I curse under my breath as Emmy laughs. "No worries, the good part about this sport is the dogs love chasing even if they don't get to catch. Try it again."

When Meadow brings the disc back, I line up, determined to do a better job. At least Stevie isn't wrapped up in Jude's arms now. But from the looks of her unbalanced, tilting throw, she might be again soon.

Wonderful.

"Can I get you a beer?" I ask Emmy and Jude about an hour later.

We'd caught a ride with Jude to Station 26 Brewing Company. Stevie and I had planned to run Bean home and grab my car, but he'd offered to drive us and Emmy there. She lives within walking distance of the park too. The rest of the club gathers with their dogs at a couple of picnic tables.

"Thanks, man," Jude says. "I'll take an IPA."

"I'll have the blonde," Emmy says.

"Same for me," Stevie says after checking the menu. "And can you get a water for Bean? I didn't think to bring any to the park."

Bean has stopped panting, but she's lying at Stevie's feet, probably ready for a drink and a snooze. Emmy brought a bowl and water for Meadow, and Bean has already drunk her fair share of it.

"That'll be ten bucks and a foot massage later," I say in a low voice in Stevie's ear.

"Not on your life. I'm not touching those hairy toes now or ever. Here's some cash, though." She digs in the back pocket of her denim shorts.

I wave her off. We share expenses equally, and when we go out, we take turns paying. It might be my turn, it might not, but we'd decided long ago that it all comes out in the wash.

I buy the pints of beer and the water and head back to the table to find Stevie sandwiched between Jude and a woman who I think is named Chloe. There's a spot next to Emmy on the other side of the table, so I take it after distributing the beverages. I pet Bean's head under the table as I put water in a plastic bowl in front of her, but she doesn't even look up. She's pooped.

Emmy's talking to Aaron, a short and muscular black guy I met today. It was his dog Bear that I almost hit with the frisbee. They glance at me as I sit down.

"Logan, right?" Aaron asks me.

"That's it," I say.

"And what's your girlfriend's name?"

I'm distracted by setting my pint glass down on a crack in the picnic table and having to grab it before it tips over. "Stevie," I say without thinking.

"Oh—I didn't realize you two were together," Emmy says. "She introduced you as her housemate."

"What?" I rewind what I'd said. My face heats up. "Oh, no, Stevie and I are friends. I . . . uh, didn't hear you right."

Emmy's gaze stays on me for a second, but Aaron takes my explanation in stride. "Well, glad you two joined the club. We need some new blood. Bear and I get tired of making Emmy and Meadow look bad all the time."

She smiles sweetly at him and I laugh. Even to a novice like me, it's already pretty clear who the best thrower and catcher in the club are.

"How long have you been doing this?" I ask them.

Aaron answers first. "Bear and I joined last year. He was so bored at home while I worked all day, he needed something active to do in the evenings other than a short walk."

His dog lifts his head when he hears his name, then his head drops back down. He's a big dog, brown and black in color with triangular-shaped ears that stay up and alert most of the time. Some sort of German shepherd mix, I guess. Bear looks as strong as his owner.

"What about you and Meadow?" I ask Emmy.

She reaches down and pets her slim, black and white border collie, who stares up at her mistress adoringly. "We've been playing with discs since she was a puppy."

"It shows."

"Thanks," she smiles at me again, and I can't help noticing how pretty, straight, and white her teeth are against her creamy tan complexion. "I taught Jude to work with her, too, so if I was busy after work, she still got her training."

"What do you do for work?" I ask them.

"I'm a yoga teacher," Emmy says, "and I work at Starbucks."

"Caffeine and chill," Aaron says.

She nods. "It's a good mix. My heart is with wellness and yoga, but Starbucks has consistent hours and benefits, so." She shrugs.

As Aaron tells me about his engineering job, my gaze slides briefly to Stevie and Jude. She's leaning close to him, listening to him talk about the last time the club competed. I keep my eyes on her for a second, hoping hers will meet mine.

They don't.

"Bean is Stevie's dog, right?" Emmy asks. A second passes before I realize she's talking to me.

I turn away from Stevie and Jude. "That's right. She got her as a puppy, but because we live together, we sort of share her."

"That's cool of you to come out and learn the disc thing with her, then," Aaron says. "My housemate can't even fill Bear's water bowl, much less throw a frisbee for him."

I smile, accepting the compliment, but my eyes sneak back to Stevie. Did she hear that? Because I don't have to be here, supporting her and Bean.

The problem is, I don't want to be anywhere else, either. Wherever Stevie is, is where I want to be.

I only wish she felt the same way.

Chapter Seven

Stevie

"Are you busy tonight?" I yell to Logan through his closed bathroom door. It's Saturday, early evening, and he's showering after his run. I can't see him, obviously, but I hear the water crashing against the shower walls.

"What?" he shouts back. I yell my question again. "No!"

"Want to go to Mom and Lamar's with me?"

"Dinner?" I think he said something else, but I'm not sure.

"Yes!"

"Okay!"

And that's how, about an hour later as the sun sets over City Park to the west, we end up walking together to my parents' home. They live about a fifteen-minute walk away, and if I'm anticipating having a drink, I stroll instead of driving. Instead of Logan driving, that is.

We could bike instead, but Bean's with us. She jogs a bit ahead, at the end of her leash, looking pretty happy. I'd given her a bath today, and unlike a lot of dogs, she loves being clean and brushed. Of course, I'd fed her plenty of treats out of her disc too. She's enjoying her disc "training" very much.

Logan's stomach snarls beside me. I laugh. "Hungry?"

"No, I'm good," Logan says, then after a pause, he adds, "So, what's Lamar making tonight?"

He knows my Mom doesn't cook. Or at least, not since she met Lamar. My stepfather is a foodie and a talented home chef. He's also a crack Trivial Pursuit player, a savvy investor, and a snappy dresser. But I'd say cooking is his superpower.

"I don't know. He didn't say." I hide my grin. I'm keeping the meal a secret until we get there.

"What did you do today?" Logan asks. "Other than giving Bean a spa treatment."

"I took Jazzy to see the new Disney princess movie, which thank god wasn't awful, and I hung out with Mom and Lamar for a few hours after that. Oh, and this morning, Bean and I threw the disc around at the park with Jude, Emmy, and Meadow."

Logan eyes me. "Really? They happened to be there at the same time?"

I snort. "No, of course not. They invited Bean and me to train with them and Meadow."

"You but not me, huh?"

I glance over. My friend looks . . . hurt? "Did you want to go? You totally could have. I'm sorry I didn't ask you. You were gone, but I should have texted."

"No, it's fine. I was joking."

He doesn't sound like he's joking. Genuinely confused, I peep at him again to try and read his expression. As I do, I step into the cross-street in front of us, and with a swift grab at my arm, Logan pulls me back. I yelp and yank Bean out of the street as the Toyota I didn't see heading our way goes by.

Logan sighs. "Stevie, I hate to have to say this, but you should really look both ways before crossing the street."

I agree, when I can finally breathe again. He's right, and it's not the only thing I *should* do. I should floss more, clean the house more, work during the day and sleep at night more, and dress and act more like an adult. My brain doesn't seem to follow the same pathways as most people. But I don't say all of that.

I lay my hand on Logan's arm instead. "Thanks."

"You're welcome." He wraps my fingers around his bicep and adds jokingly, "Now hold my hand while we cross the street."

A feather runs up my own arm, or at least that's what it feels like, but I ignore the old, familiar sensation that I get when Logan touches me. I ignore it because he's my oldest, best, and occasionally solitary friend. And nothing else.

Mom and Lamar's home in South Park Hill is a gorgeous two-story brick Denver square on an oversized lot with beautiful, lush landscaping. The house is perfectly maintained, and the yard could be the green of a fancy golf course. I ring the doorbell. No one answers, but music drifts from the fenced back yard, so we head around back.

Their yard is my favorite part of the home. It's wide and deep with a circular stone patio, a built-in fireplace and grill, and several shade trees, one with a long rope swing for Jazzy and another with a hammock. I'd spent many a happy afternoon in that hammock napping, reading, or borrowing their Netflix back when I couldn't afford my own account.

Mom reclines on a lounger on the patio, talking on the phone. She waves at us excitedly and gestures toward the open French doors at the back of the house. I pull a bottle of wine from my backpack and wave it at Mom with a questioning look. She points to her already full glass of red. I give her a thumbs up.

Logan makes a noise. "Ah ha. There *is* a secret language between mothers and daughters. I think I read an article about it in *Popular Science*."

I snort. "More likely you saw us in *Wine Enthusiast*." I poke my head in the doorway. A delicious, seafoody scent wafts to my nostrils. "Lamar?"

A deep voice rumbles from the kitchen. "C'mon in."

I take Bean off her leash to go sniff around the yard, knowing Mom will keep an eye on her, and step inside, inhaling deeply.

Lamar, his waist wrapped in an apron, stirs an enormous pot on the cooktop. Inside, the thick, bubbling stew is a lovely fiery color. Bits of shredded chicken, shrimp, and vegetables like celery, onion, and peppers breach the surface as he stirs. I hug my stepfather, relishing his bear-like embrace. He's always given the greatest hugs.

"Hello there, co-conspirator," he says.

"Mmm," Logan breathes in appreciatively. He peeks in the pot, too. "What is this deliciousness?"

I turn to him, grinning. "Traditional gumbo, straight from Grandma Celia's kitchen. Secret ingredients and all. And I made it."

Logan freezes for a second, then smiles. "Number eight on the bucket list: check."

"Yep. With some help." I squeeze Lamar's side before letting him go.

"She did all the hard work." He pats my back. "Made the roux, chopped, measured, stirred, and mixed."

Logan smirks. "And . . . is it edible?"

My stepfather glowers at him. "Of course it's edible. No inedible food is prepared in *this* kitchen, son."

They're both joking. Well, not Lamar so much. But definitely Logan. My friend hugs my stepfather after I let him go. Logan's about six inches taller than Lamar, but they've always seemed to see eye to eye, nonetheless.

"Aren't you proud of her?" Lamar asks him.

"Definitely," Logan says, but I can read the uncertainty in his eyes, I guess about my cooking skills. I'm a little hurt, but I hide it.

"I promise it's going to be delicious," I say. Then, I ask Lamar, "Where do we want to set up?"

"Outside, I thought."

He reaches up to the cabinets to get plates, which I wait to take from him. Logan heads for the utensil drawer. As I carry the dishes outside, Jazzy barrels into the backyard from the side gate, calling for Bean. My dog looks up from the bush she had her head stuck in and runs to greet my niece. The resulting kid and dog hug is reminiscent of a military homecoming. It's like they haven't seen each other in years.

Mom lays her phone down on the side table and stands. "Sorry, everyone. I had some clients who needed to be talked off the ledge about the contract they're about to sign."

She hugs me, then Logan, who stepped out of the kitchen behind me, waves to Tamara and Dean, and when Jazzy untangles herself from Bean, Mom twirls her granddaughter around in a grandma greeting.

"Oh, I'm so happy you all can be here. I love having my family around!" Mom says.

We laugh. My mother isn't shy about expressing her feelings, that's for sure. I glance at Logan. He's looking at me, his expression hard to read again. But when I smile, he smiles back.

We all catch up on our weeks as we help bring the food to the table. I'd made a green salad earlier to go with the stew, and Lamar had bought and warmed crusty, fresh French bread to serve as well. When we finally tuck into the meal, I realize I did an okay job on the gumbo. The dish might be missing some of the culinary magic Lamar sprinkles into his own food, but it's thick, rich, and perfectly seasoned, according to Tamara, who's eaten her dad's gumbo since . . . maybe not birth, but soon after. Even Jazzy, whose meal consisted of a dollop of gumbo beside small piles of shredded chicken, vegetables, and fruit, takes a taste and declares it "not that icky."

"Thank you again for teaching me, Lamar," I say after everyone compliments the flavor.

He smiles and raises his wine glass to me. "I was pleased to help check it off the list."

The sun has set, casting the patio in shadows. Mom lights a few candles on the table which add to the festive feel. After finishing the meal, we chat about Tamara and Dean's Adventure Thursday kayaking trip last week and their visit to some hot

A.G. HENLEY

springs in the Collegiate Peaks area near Salida a few days ago, Jazzy's movie date with me, and a new restaurant downtown that Lamar and Mom tried last night.

"What have you been up to, Logan?" Mom asks. "We haven't seen you in a few weeks."

"Working, running, gaming. The usual," he says. "I've also been going to the disc dogs club meeting with Stevie and Bean."

"That's right," Mom says. "Stevie, you said you'd show us what she's learned."

"Ooh, yes." I grab the tooth marked disc out of my backpack, along with a packet of peanut butter in case Bean needs extra motivation. Although only a week or two old, the disc already has puncture marks and the beginning of a crack in the rim. Jude and Emmy had warned me that discs made for dogs were notoriously short-lived. Depending on how often dogs play with them, and how soft or hard they bite the disc, the cheaper ones last a few weeks and the pricey varieties about a month. Jude had advised me to stock up if I ever saw them on sale.

Bean, who'd sat in the grass during dinner keeping a watchful eye out for the scraps that inevitably came her way from Jazzy, jumps up, her tail wagging when she sees the disc.

I smear a little peanut butter on the edge of it and let her sniff but not lick it. "Ready to work, girl?"

I wave the disc around slowly in front of her face. Then, using my new throwing technique that Jude taught me, I spin the disc into the corner of the yard near the hammock. Bean tears off through the grass and with a quick glance back over her shoulder, turns and catches it neatly in her mouth.

My family applauds. Jazzy scrambles out of her chair. "I want to throw for her! Can I throw for her, Aunt Stevie?"

"Of course." I give Bean the order to bring the disc back, but she hasn't quite gotten that down yet, so I retrieve it myself. Then I hand it to Jazzy, who tries to replicate what I did. We wipe more peanut butter on the disc's edge, she lets Bean sniff it,

48

THE CONUNDRUM OF COLLIES

and throws. It lands about two feet away. Jazzy—and Bean—look so disappointed, we all chuckle. Tears fill my niece's eyes.

"Don't laugh," she says.

I squat beside her. "We're aren't laughing at you, sweet pea, only at Bean."

Jazzy pouts. "She doesn't like being laughed at, either."

"You're probably right. I'm sorry." I snuggle her for a moment and then reach to pick up the disc. "Let me show you how to throw this thing."

I kneel, and putting my arm around Jazzy, slowly show her the movement, the way Jude did with me at the park. It had been helpful to learn exactly how to hold the frisbee and how to keep everything level, so it flies straight.

"Got it?" I scoot back.

Jazzy's eyes narrow with determination, and her full lips purse. "Ready."

Bean runs as Jazzy curls her arm and throws. The frisbee goes twice as far this time. It lands in the grass, but Bean quickly circles back and scoops it up when Jazzy tells her to. We all clap.

"Well done, Jazz," Dean says. "And Stevie, it's amazing that Bean already gets the gist of this."

I grin, proud of her. When Jazzy lines up to throw for Bean again, I stay with her to help correct her wind up and throw. Behind us, the conversation at the table turns to other things. After a couple more tosses, I hear my name.

"Thirty," Mom says. "I really can't believe it. How's it going with the list?" I can tell she's lowering her voice intentionally, but it doesn't quite work. Although my mother is a lot of things, quiet isn't one of them.

Hot blood creeps up my neck and burns my ears. Why does my family ask Logan things about me? We're close, but why would he know more about my life than I do? Then again, maybe he does. Maybe I should keep listening and learn something about myself.

"And you," Mom says, "I can't believe you're already thirty. It seems like yesterday that you were peeing in the corner of our backyard because you didn't want to stop playing and come inside to use the bathroom."

Everyone laughs, including me, although I smother it.

Then Logan says, "*I'm* having trouble believing I'm thirty and still solidly single."

Mom makes an *mmm* noise of understanding. "That can be remedied, Logan Stephens."

The conversation moves on, but I chew on what I'd heard. Logan sounded unhappy about being single. Like he's lonely.

And who can blame him, living with me? He probably feels like he's sharing a house with a disorganized vampire or something. I work all night and sleep during the day, I'm a terrible housekeeper, I'm pretty moody, and my dental hygiene definitely needs work. Logan deserves a loving, kind, smart, beautiful, organized, mature woman.

A woman like—

And that's when I have my best idea yet. I'd thought joining the Denver Disc Dogs would only check item number seven off my list. Now? I'm gunning for number one.

I want to *change someone's life for the better*, and I'm determined that someone will be Logan. And I know exactly who can help me do it.

Emmy.

Chapter Eight

Logan

"Bean, don't even think about it," Stevie says in a warning voice.

I glance over the top of my iPad at the dog. Bean hunches and wags the tip of her tail, looking guilty.

"She was trying to scratch around the pavers," Stevie tells me.

We're sitting at our round metal patio table the morning after the gumbo feast, drinking coffee and reading in the shade of the faded and half-broken umbrella over our heads. Well, I'm reading. Stevie is sketching, one of her favorite hobbies.

Ever since we were kids, she'd doodled in notebooks, on scraps of paper, and sometimes on me. I had to throw out a favorite pair of jeans in high school when she'd doodled on my leg.

After Bean got to Rosa's chickens the other night, we'd stuffed several pavers into the hole in the fence. Now Bean's trying to finagle a way around it. The hens next door squawk softly, a constant temptation. From Bean's point of view, they're in constant danger of wandering off and getting lost.

"Moe needs to actually fix the fence," I say referring to our landlord. "Along with the hall closet door, the water damage in the ceiling in my room, and the floor gouge in the living room."

She groans. "Maybe we should move out."

"Or . . . maybe we should buy a house."

I keep my voice casual and wait for a response, still pretending to read. Stevie keeps her eyes on Bean, who's moved on to sniffing other likely spots in the fence.

"I don't know," she finally says. "We can't even keep up with this place."

My heart, which had started to beat a little faster when she didn't immediately shoot my idea down, sags in my chest.

My friend and unintentional tormentress looks casually beautiful this morning. She's still wearing her pajamas—a pair of worn flannel pants and a T-shirt—and her hair is a wild pile on top of her head. But the sun gleams off the blonde strands, and her blue eyes glint when she has a new idea as she draws, and her mouth twitches while she tries to recreate whatever image is in her head. I wish, a lot more often than I should, that I could touch those lips—

Stevie slams her notebook shut, making me jump and Bean jerk around to see what happened. I blink, feeling inexplicably guilty, as if she could hear my thoughts and didn't approve. At all.

"Let's go for a run," she says. "Do you want to go for a run?"

"Um, what?" I stutter.

"Run. You know, that sweaty activity you do almost every day."

In other words, exercise. Also known as number nine on her list. "Oh, *run*. I thought you said bun. I was wondering if you meant like you wanted a cinnamon bun or a burger bun or maybe a hot crossed bun. I thought we'd be walking to Cake Crumbs." Which is a terrific little bakery right here in Park Hill.

She groans at my bad joke. "I'll go put my running shoes on. Maybe some exercise will chase the fowl-minded thoughts out of Bean."

I stare at her, barely registering the pun. "Running shoes? You don't own running shoes."

She grins and tilts her head, holding her notebook against her chest like a schoolgirl. "Shows you how much you know. I went to Denver Running Company and got a pair this week."

"What kind?"

"Um . . . Brooks? I think."

I nod. "A solid choice. Where do you want to go?"

"Let's start with City Park. I don't know how long I'll make it. I might even collapse before we get where we're going."

"If you do, I'll carry you home. I never leave a woman behind." As I say it, I really try not to let my thoughts dwell on Stevie's, uh, behind.

"Glad to know that. I feel better already." She hitches her pajama pants up, but not before I glimpse a sliver of smooth, pale skin below her shirt and above the trim of her panties.

I bury my nose in the Sunday *New York Times* article about turtles in the Indian Ocean for another minute before going to change myself. Fascinating things, turtles. So ancient. So deliberate and non-spontaneous. So . . . not tantalizing. Unlike Stevie.

As my housemate picks up her coffee mug, calls to Bean, and pads inside, I think she might actually be killing me. Not intentionally. Just by being herself.

And if she'd realize that she loves me as much as I love her—well then, I'd die a happy man.

Chapter Nine

Stevie

Logan and I meet in the living room about ten minutes after I suggested the run. Bean stands between us, her head turning one way and then another, clearly getting the message we're going somewhere. I don't have her harness or leash, but somehow, she knows anyway. Dogs always know.

Logan looks me up and down and frowns. "Are you . . . sure you're ready?"

He wears his usual running garb: thin running shorts, one of those shirts that wicks sweat away or whatever, and his expensive running shoes, the one thing he's always willing to spend a lot of money on. I check myself out. I'm in a pair of pajama shorts, a cotton T-shirt, and my new shoes.

"Is this not okay?" I ask.

He squints. "It's fine, but if you like running, you might want to invest in some clothes made from sweat wicking fabrics."

I snort and head for the door. "This isn't going to last long enough for me to sweat anyway. I expect I'll pass out after half a mile."

He laughs. "I doubt it. You're fit from all the walking and bike riding you do. Jogging won't be a big jump."

Ohhhh, how wrong he is. A little more than one half-mile into the jaunt, I'm ready to faint. Death is clearly the next step.

"I . . . have . . . to . . . walk," I say as we reach the fountain behind the museum. At least I'll die in City Park. Could be worse.

I put my hands on my knees, panting, and then slump onto a bench. Bean stops and looks at me. She's panting, too, but she wasn't having any trouble at all keeping up with Logan. As for my friend, he slows his easy pace, walks back to Bean and me, and sits beside me. He puts his arm across the back, not really even breathing hard.

"You . . . suck," I say.

He pats my shoulder in response, and I cringe at the sweat he probably came into contact with. Cotton T-shirts, I've learned, do not wick. They soak.

While Logan scans the view of the mountains, and I try not to actually perish, a couple of families enjoy the fountain beside us. It's one of those features that randomly shoots sprays of water into the air, and the kids run through them. In this case, six kids are fully suited up in bathing suits and one even wears goggles and a set of water wings for some reason. Bean lies at our feet and watches them, too.

Logan chuckles as one of the kids shrieks. A spray apparently hit a little guy square in the face. It must not have hurt because the boy laughs delightedly. The girl with water wings refuses to get wet at all. She stands at the side, watching. Why do I have a feeling that would have been me back in the day?

"You okay?" Logan asks me.

I sigh. "Why did I think I could do this?"

"Getting into running is always hard. And although we stretched a little, and you *are* in decent shape, it takes some time for your legs to adjust."

"Like how long?"

"A few weeks, maybe?"

I groan. "Weeks?"

"If running was easy and unceasingly enjoyable, everyone would do it."

I throw an arm out at the joggers, runners, and speed walkers going by. "It looks like everyone in Denver *does* do it."

"C'mon," Logan says, patting me. "We'll walk for a while and then go again. The run-walk strategy works for a lot of new runners."

I stand. My legs feel like a pair of melting popsicles, but they hold my weight. Bean jumps up, ready to go.

"You suck, too," I mutter at her.

"Let's head this way," Logan says, starting to jog. "I want to show you something."

I follow, already intensely regretting adding item number nine to my bucket list. He leads me down a path along the edge of the park that borders the zoo.

"We should . . . go to the zoo soon," I pant. "We haven't been . . . in a long time."

"Like years," Logan says easily.

"Maybe . . . invite Emmy and Jude," I say. "I like them. Don't you?"

He hesitates, but then quickly answers yes. Huh. I stop running. It's been a minute; time to walk. Logan slows, too.

"Wait, *do* you like them?" I ask when I can. "I think they've been so great about helping us at the club meetings. Bean wouldn't have gotten nearly as far as she has without them."

He nods. "Yep, they're great." He doesn't sound enthusiastic until he adds, "Especially Emmy."

My heart does a funny flip flop, which I take as excitement. He's playing directly into my plan. "I don't have to invite Jude."

He runs a hand through his not-even-the-least-bit-sweaty hair. "No, no. Invite him. He's a good guy."

I brighten. "I think so, too. Sweet—I'll see when they're free. Where are we going, by the way?"

"Here." Logan gestures to the little lake that sits between the park and the wall around the zoo. Tons of birds are always in and around it, and people feeding and watching the birds along the edges. Which brings the squirrels, pigeons, and ants. It's a zoo out here, too, come to think of it.

Today's no different. We stand beside the water and watch feathered friends go about their business. Bean looks like she wishes she could round them all up, so I hold her leash tightly. The last thing wild animals need is for Bean to chase them. Chickens are bad enough.

"Are we looking at something in particular?" I ask.

Logan points to a tall gray bird with a bright orange beak and pink legs. "See that goose? She's really unusual. This species usually lives in Eurasia, but occasionally they can be found other places, like . . . here."

I moan. "Not another bird lesson."

My friend's expression slips from eager to carefully neutral. "Okay. No more. Sorry."

As he walks away, I grab his arm. It slips through my grasp until I'm holding his hand. "I'm sorry, Logan. I was teasing. I like learning about the birds. Truly."

I catch his eyes, too, apologizing with my gaze. He's seen my sorry face often enough over a lifetime of friendship, that's for sure. "What species is this?"

He half-smiles, a lopsided look that is his *apology accepted* expression. "A graylag goose. And his mate should be around here somewhere, too. Like a lot of geese, they mate for life." We search the lake, but no other geese match. Logan's eyebrows pinch. "Maybe she's out feeding."

"What's so cool about the graylags, other than that they're lost?" I joke.

"Well, an ocean and half a continent away from home is pretty darn lost, for one thing. These must have gone rogue. Usually they live in flocks for protection. And sometimes they help raise other goslings. Occasionally the pairs are even two males instead of males and females."

"Really?"

He nods. "It's a lot more common in animals than people think."

"So, where's this one's mate?"

Logan shrugs. "She was here last week before we met for the club. I spotted them on my run."

We watch the graylag as he struts around in the grass. With the length of his neck and the stern set of his beak, he's rather regal.

I mess with the loop at the top of Bean's leash. "What happens when a goose dies?"

"It goes to goose heaven. Or if it was particularly naughty, goose hell." He hadn't even missed a beat.

I elbow him. "I mean to its mate."

"Sometimes the survivor will mate with another goose. But I doubt that would be possible for this one. He lives too far from other graylags."

"He'd be alone."

He glances at me again. "Yeah. Geese really grieve their mates when they die, too. Even when they lose eggs, they grieve."

A lump grows in my throat as I watch the lone goose. Which is ridiculous. We don't even know if his mate is gone. She's probably out feeding, like Logan said. Or exercising. Heck, maybe she's making gumbo or flossing her . . . beak. But tears still well in my eyes.

Logan puts an arm around me. "She'll be back." He squeezes me before letting me go. "Maybe we can jog again this week and come back and check on them."

"That sounds good. Wait," I smack my forehead, "nothing about jogging sounds good."

He chortles. "Want to go a little farther or are you done?"

Bean stares at me, wagging her tail encouragingly.

My chin sinks to my chest. "A *little* farther. But if I fall out, take Bean and keep going. Leave me where I lie. Promise me, Logan." I say this dramatically while clutching the hem of his shirt.

He brushes hair down on the top of my head. "I told you. I never leave a woman behind."

"And that's why you're my oldest and best friend."

Friends . . . I suddenly think, and friends only. No matter how wonderful he is. No matter how comfortable we are together, how well we get along, how much fun we can have doing not much of anything at all.

Because if I want all those things to stay true, I know that friends are all we ever can be.

Chapter Ten

Logan

The next week at club, Jude teaches Stevie and Bean their first freestyle trick. I hang out with Emmy, helping throw the disc for Meadow, while Jude shows Stevie the basics of how to train Bean to do things like leap in the air and gently grab a frisbee out of her hand.

Competitions, we've learned, have both throw and catch events, like most of the dogs in the club practice, and freestyle events, where the human and dog perform a complicated set of moves, kind of like ice dancing. But on land with a dog, a disc, and no ice. If that makes any sense. The human strikes different poses and holds or gently spins the disc while the dog leaps, climbs, and runs to grab them.

At least this time Jude doesn't have to put his hands all over Stevie. I thump myself mentally. Even if he does put his hands all over her, it's none of my business. I repeat that to myself. *None of my business.* Yet, anyway.

"Logan?" Emmy looks at me as if I missed something she said. I focus on her face. On her pretty face. On her *very* pretty face.

Her tea-brown eyes are almond shaped, and her shiny dark-brown hair is pulled back into a loose braid. She's wearing one of those tight-fitting sports dresses that show her lean arms and a good bit of her legs.

"Yeah, sorry. What was that?" I ask.

She tosses me the disc. "I asked if you wanted a turn."

"Sure, thanks." I line myself up and spin the frisbee out. Meadow races across the grass and catches it as it comes down, timing her arrival and grab perfectly. She looks pleased with herself as she carries it back to me.

"Do you and Meadow win *all* competitions or only *most* of them?" I ask teasingly.

Emmy answers the question seriously. "Meadow's a state and regional champion, and I've been thinking about taking her to worlds. I think she could do well there. She's really disciplined and focused, you know?" She laughs. It's a sweet, tinkling sound, like a spoon tapped against a champagne glass. "Is it bragging if I'm talking about my dog?"

"I don't think it's bragging when you're being factual, and I asked. Although, Meadow couldn't do this without you. You're both champions."

"I guess that's true." Emmy smiles and toys with the treat bag she carries. Of all the dogs, Meadow seems the least interested in food rewards and most motivated by the joy of chasing the disc, but Emmy reinforces the joy through Meadow's stomach.

"When's the next competition?" I ask after throwing the disc again. My spins are not as good as Emmy's. They don't go as far, stay on as straight of a path, or dip as smoothly and with the right timing as hers or the others in the club do.

"End of August," she says. "It's in Littleton. Sometimes we travel to Fort Collins or Colorado Springs, and there's a fun one up in the mountains in Avon every summer, but this one is here in the Denver metro. I think Bean's ready if Stevie wants to compete."

I pause to watch Stevie and Bean for a minute. They're

getting better quickly, but Bean's nowhere near Meadow, Bear, or a few of the other dogs' levels. They've been at this a lot longer, after all.

I must look doubtful, because Emmy adds, "There are novice, intermediate, and advanced divisions, plus a freestyle competition. Bean would do great with the novices."

"Oh, in that case, I have a feeling she would." As we watch, Bean trots back with the disc in her mouth and tries to give it to Stevie. She's too involved in something she's telling Jude to take it from her, even after Bean knocks it against her leg.

Hands on his hips, Jude smiles and laughs, totally focused on Stevie. I wonder what she's telling him about. He's new, he's fresh, he's probably a lot more interesting to talk to. I know all her stories already.

"Logan?"

I glance at Emmy. She looks . . . sympathetic. "Do you want me to take over?"

Meadow sits at my feet with the disc, waiting for me to take it.

"No, sorry, I've got it." Turning away from Stevie and Jude, I throw Meadow's disc long and hard. And yeah, I might be picturing Jude's good-looking face as the target.

§♣

Later, over beers at Station 26, I sit beside Aaron and an Indian woman from the club named Nisha. This is the first time she's come to a workout since Stevie and I joined, although she said she's been a member since moving to Denver two years ago to do her residency in internal medicine at the nearby University of Colorado Hospital.

Her dog, a white and brown Australian shepherd mix named Jack, had barked excitedly every time she threw the disc for him. But now, like the others, he's laid out under the table snoozing.

Nisha tells me her name means *night* in Sanskrit. "Which is appropriate," she jokes, "because as a resident I work all night. And all day for that matter."

She tells us a story about a patient she had this week who had a mysterious set of symptoms that he was convinced was leprosy, even though none of the symptoms matched. "I'm pretty sure he was disappointed when I told him it wasn't leprosy, and more likely to be a virus. Or maybe hypochondriasis."

Aaron and I laugh. I glance down the table at Jude, Emmy, and Stevie. Bean is at Stevie's feet, a bowl of water in front of her tired nose, and her gaze focused on some squirrels chasing each other around a nearby tree. How can the dog still be interested in running after small animals after all the running after frisbees she did this evening?

"What do you do, Logan?" Aaron asks me.

"I'm an accountant." When they both nod, I joke, "And that's usually the end of *that* conversation." They chuckle. "Not the most exciting of careers, unfortunately, although I enjoy it."

"What do you guys do for fun, other than this?" Nisha sighs. "I have no time for hobbies, much less a social life, so I live vicariously through other people."

"I like to run," I say. "And I game with friends to relax at night." I'm shy about telling people about my bird watching hobby. I shouldn't be, I know, but the humiliation lingers from a time I told a girl I liked in middle school about it and she laughed at me. And promptly told all her giggling friends.

"Me, too. Gaming, not running. I only run when chased." Aaron makes a face and then pets Bear's head when he pops up under the table to scratch an itch. "I also play the violin."

"Really?" Nisha looks interested. "I had no idea. I played the cello in high school. I've been wanting to pick it up again. We should get together for a session!"

Aaron almost chokes on his beer. "Hang on now, I didn't say I played well."

"I haven't played in like seven years! How bad could you be compared to that?"

As they talk about their music backgrounds, my attention drifts down the table again. Emmy's talking to Scott, another guy from the club, and Stevie and Jude lean in toward each other, deep in conversation.

Jealousy punches me in the gut. I have no right to be jealous. None at all. But tell that to the warty green trolls playing tackle football in my abdomen. As I watch from the corner of my eye, Bean worms her way out from under the table and flies after the squirrels by the tree, her leash trailing behind her.

Stevie squeezes out from behind the picnic table and runs after her, Jude hot on their heels. Jack and Bear leap up and bark. Bear hits his head on the underside of the table with a thump.

I grab a handful of chips from the plate of chips and salsa I bought when we got there. Stevie and Jude try to trap Bean between them, but she keeps darting away, her eyes on the tree top the squirrels escaped to.

"Bean," I say over the wild barking, "want a treat?"

She looks over, looks back at the tree, and then comes to me. I give her a chip and grasp her collar.

Stevie rewards me with a grateful smile as she collects Bean. "Why don't I ever remember the food?"

"Nice work." Jude claps me on the back. It's a friendly gesture, but I have the ridiculous urge to punch him. Then grab him by some vulnerable part of his body and mutter *stay away from her* in his ear, like some kind of meathead jealous boyfriend. Never mind that despite being a few inches shorter, he probably has twenty pounds of muscle on me.

Back at the table, beers are overturned, dogs whine, and everyone's on their feet. Which means Bean's breakout effectively breaks up the party. We all take a few more drinks of our beers and snacks, clean up, and head out.

Stevie, Bean, and I walk home. It's dark, the perfect temperature, and once we're on side streets, quiet. Walking at night feels like moving together in our own private bubble. Bean pads beside us, totally oblivious to the temporary chaos she'd caused.

"That was an exciting finish to the night," I say.

Stevie sighs. "I guess she needs more disc throwing. I'd hoped I was starting to see some change in her. A mellowing. But now I'm not so sure. Maybe I need to pay for some training or send her away to one of those doggie behavior bootcamps."

"You could, but can you really see her saluting the drill sergeant?"

She laughs, but then goes quiet. "I guess not. Then, it's up to me to help her to grow up and mature."

I glance at my old friend, not so sure she's still talking about Bean. I choose my words carefully.

"She is mature. She just . . . lives life on her own terms. And there's nothing wrong with that."

Stevie smiles at me, her eyes a little teary.

When we were in fourth grade, Stevie's teacher had given her a bad report card because of her "immature and disruptive behavior." Carol had been really upset until she spoke to the school principal, a wise older lady who'd been in education since dinosaurs roamed the earth, or so all us kids thought. She'd told Carol that although she didn't want to undermine her teaching staff, she believed that, "Your daughter just lives life on her own terms. And there's nothing wrong with that."

I didn't know any of this at the time, of course; I'm not even sure Stevie did. She'd told me much later. But she'd seemed to let the teacher's words define her in a way that still bothers her. Bothers me, too.

Like when my high school cross country coach told me I wasn't a disciplined enough runner junior year; it kept me from seriously pursuing cross country in college. Everyone has these moments, I think, where we unequivocally believe other people's judgments about us.

I want to touch my friend, to reassure her, but instead I reach down and scratch Bean's head. She looks at me and grins. Not really, but the patch of white around the underside of her jaw and up onto her muzzle makes her look like she's smiling.

"At least she hasn't chased Rosa's chickens in a few weeks," I say. "Full credit for that."

"True. Thanks to the club and Emmy and Jude's training." Stevie brushes away something off her arm. "Oh, hey, what would you say to going out with Emmy, and Jude and me this weekend?"

Emmy . . . and Jude and me. I don't like the sound of that. Like Emmy and I would be a pair, and Jude and Stevie would be another pair.

A couple of answers shoot through my brain, all with one response in common: *no*. Not unless the pairing is Stevie and me, and Emmy and Jude. Or Stevie and me, and anyone else.

But instead of that, I say yes while silently cursing my cowardice.

Chapter Eleven

Stevie

Friday afternoon I put the finishing touches on a website redesign that I've been working on all week for a local restaurant. I'm particularly proud of this one. The design is simple but fresh, the colors pop, and best of all, I managed to do most of it before midnight each day for the last week.

I've been inching my bedtime up by half an hour every day. Before this week, it wasn't weird at all for me to still be working at dawn, so midnight is a major improvement. I decide to celebrate finishing the website and working hard to accomplish number four on my list, *establish a healthy work-life balance*, by cleaning my room.

Cleaning can't be high on anyone's list of ways to celebrate things, mine included. But I'm on a roll and tackling two items on my bucket list in one day is way too exciting a prospect to pass up.

I tackle my tangled bed first, starting with stripping my sheets and washing them, along with my comforter, something that doesn't happen nearly as often as it should. Then, I move on to cleaning out my nightstands—how old are these lip balms??—

and then my closet and chest of drawers. That's not as much of a challenge, thanks to my skimpy wardrobe.

My desk, however, is another story.

I face it, hands on my head. I haven't cleaned out my desk in . . . I don't want to think about how long. The tabletop is about five feet wide with a hutch thingy on top and several drawers below. I have two file cabinets overflowing with contracts and other paperwork, and my Wall of Inspiration, a huge whiteboard that I use as a physical Pinterest of sorts, covered in drawings, snippets of magazines, and paper stuck on with magnets, is mounted on the wall over the file cabinets.

I often sketch out my ideas on the Wall of Inspiration before I do any computer work. Over the course of a few projects, it can get pretty crowded. I rarely take the time to really clean up the Wall or my desk, so things tend to stack up.

With a deep, settling breath, I take everything off my desk, including my MacBook Pro and printer, and pile it on my naked mattress. To the bed, I add my sketch pads, file folders, pens, pencils, markers, thinking yoyo, and, teetering on top, my plants. I have to have some green on my desk.

Next, I pull everything off my Wall and make a couple of neat piles. A lot of the piles can be recycled or go into my finished project file folders. This really shouldn't take that long.

But. It's like walking down a few months or even years' worth of work memories.

Tam and I once dug out an old photo album at Mom and Lamar's house, searching for a particular picture. We ended up on the floor hours later with about ten albums open around us, glasses of wine in hand, laughing and almost in tears. This is a little like that.

And that's why Logan finds me, when he gets home from work, lying on my back on the floor with Bean, both of us surrounded by finished logos, sketches, invoices, magazine scraps, and manila folders. A glass of wine, thrice emptied, is on the nearest side table.

Logan's wearing one of his cute little preppy collared shirts with a tie and slacks. His leather messenger bag is on his shoulder, and he smells slightly spicy.

"Hi, you," I giggle.

He sighs. "Stevie. You said last time that you wouldn't clean your desk when I wasn't home. You promised."

"Oh, yeah." I honestly hadn't remembered promising that until he said it. "I'm sorry. It's been a long time."

And it had. Probably about three years. He'd found me then, about like now, surrounded by the paper bird droppings of my work life, drinking and pretending to sort things out.

"We were going to run."

I slide my head so I can see him better. "We can. Give me ten minutes."

He rolls his eyes. "Stevie, you're three drinks into the weekend and your room looks like a hurricane blew about thirteen hundred miles off course and hit right here. I don't think a run is going to happen."

I stumble to my feet, chagrined. "I . . . I'm sorry."

He sets his bag down with a heavy thump. "C'mon, let's get this mess cleaned up."

When he looks at me, something like pity—or is it disgust? —suffuses his face. I stiffen. It's one thing for me to pity him for having to live with me. It's another for him to pity me for being, well, me.

"No thanks," I say. "I've got it. You go for your run."

Logan grabs a dust cloth I'd brought in hours ago to clean the desk with but never got around to using. "It's okay. Let me help."

"No." I take the cloth out of his hand. "But thanks."

His lips thin, something they do when he's annoyed. And he's rarely ever annoyed with anyone but me. Who can blame him?

"Stevie. Don't be an ass."

"I'm not being an *ass*. I'm trying to clean my room. Thank you for offering to help. Now, if you'll excuse me, I have a few years of crap to clean up."

He closes his eyes, muttering something. "Fine. See you later." He snatches his bag off the ground, turns, and stalks out.

I groan to myself. Five hours ago, I had such good intentions. What happened?

What usually happens. *I* happened. I always happen.

Most people's bucket lists are full of cool, exotic trips or once in a lifetime experiences. Mine consists of cleaning my freaking room and occasionally the spaces between my teeth. And I can't even do those things without getting buzzed and triggering a pity response in my best friend.

Stupid Stevie. Stupid, stupid Stevie.

With a rush of anger, all aimed at myself, I take another swig of wine, prepare the dust cloth and take it out on the years of dust piled up on my desk.

Two hours, and two more glasses of wine later, I finish. My desk is clean and organized, every sheet of paper and writing utensil has a home, my keyboard is free of smudges, my monitor sparkles, my bed is made with clean linens, and I'm . . . exhausted.

As I'd worked, I heard Logan call for Bean to take her on his run, they'd come back, he'd showered, and he'd banged around in the kitchen. He hadn't offered to make me anything to eat like he usually would.

I'd had plenty of time and enough grapes to get my guilt juices flowing. Logan had offered to help. He hadn't said one critical word. Then again, he hadn't needed to. I can read my best friend's face perfectly well, thank you.

My whole life, I've been very sensitive to criticism. I know every fault I have. Could catalogue them for you at any moment. I don't need anyone to point them out. But Logan hadn't pointed anything out. He'd only looked disappointed.

I creep out to the living room, empty wine bottle and glass in one hand, a fistful of apologies in the other. He's on the couch playing a game, back to me, headphones on. After a quick detour to the sink and recycle bin, I pad into the living room, Bean on my heels, and sit on the couch beside Logan. She curls up in her dog bed by the gas fireplace that doesn't work.

My housemate doesn't look at me or even acknowledge me. He's playing one of his first-person shooter games, and he must be playing by himself, because he's not talking to anyone through the headset.

I watch for a while, and then I slide a little closer and put my head on his shoulder. He doesn't make room, doesn't even move. It's like I'm not there.

For a second.

Then, he pauses his game and slides an arm around my shoulders. I wrap my arms around his torso and hug him fiercely.

"I'm sorry," I whisper into his chest.

Logan has a very nicely toned chest. I'm trying to ignore that fact as my face is pressed against it with merely his thin white cotton T-shirt between us. He squeezes my shoulder. His way of telling me it's okay.

"I don't deserve you as a bestie," I say.

"I know."

I wait for him to say more, but he doesn't, so I poke him hard in the ribs. He yelps, puts me in a neck hold, and rubs his knuckles against my scalp, something he's done since we were kids arguing in the backyard.

"Stop!" I yell. He does, and I push him away. "Jerk." I don't mean it and he knows it.

"Room done?" He restarts his game.

I nod. "I was going to do the whole house by the time you got home, surprise you, but . . ." My voice trails off. I don't have to explain, not to him.

"Why wouldn't you let me help?" He sounds hurt.

"Because, Logan, I'm almost thirty years old. I should be able to handle cleaning my room by now. Shouldn't I? I mean, seriously. Shouldn't I?" I swallow hard. "Number six on my bucket list is to clean the whole house and keep it organized. I can't even clean my own *room*. What's wrong with me?"

Logan listens quietly, his face grave, then squeezes me again. "Nothing's wrong with you, Stevie. Nothing at all."

He's lying, but for once, I don't argue. It's not his problem to figure out. It's mine.

And I swear I'll do it.

Chapter Twelve

Logan

Despite my overwhelming desire not to see Stevie on what sounds suspiciously like a date with Jude, somehow, I'm still walking to the zoo with her on Saturday evening.

First, I don't like zoos that much.

Second, I don't like Jude that much. Okay, that's not fair. Jude's fine. The problem is that *Stevie* seems to like him too much.

And third, I'm not interested in Emmy or vice versa, as far as I can tell. Any Emmy-Logan pairing seems to be a figment of Stevie's well-developed imagination.

I rub my face. This zoo date is exhausting, and we aren't even through the gates and smelling the exquisite fragrance of animal dung yet.

"What?" Stevie asks.

"What?" I look at her.

"Why did you rub your face and groan?"

Crap. I didn't know I'd groaned. I glance around looking for a groan-inducing excuse and spot a car in the zoo parking lot that we're passing. "That, uh, Mercedes has really cheesy rims."

"Rims?" She eyes me.

Did I use the right word? I'm not exactly a car guy. Aren't the things inside the tires called rims?

"Yeah, the rims." I point at the offensive car, which, now that I look more closely, has perfectly normal rims as far as I can tell. "Why?"

"I've never heard you use a word like rims. You aren't a car guy."

Exactly. Luckily, she's even less of a car girl. "Anyway, what are we doing at the zoo again?"

"Meeting Emmy and Jude."

"But, then what? Walk around, look at animals . . . flirt?" I can't resist throwing that in.

Stevie shades her eyes and looks up at me. "Why? Planning on doing a lot of that with Emmy?"

No! I want to yell. But of course, I don't. After a long look at my flat expression, she answers, "It's Safari Sunsets tonight. The zoo is open until nine and it's adults only. Which means no to kids or families and yes to adult bevvies."

I nod. "I was wondering if we'd be overrun by ankle biters."

She snorts. "Ankle biters?"

"You've never heard that term? It means kids." Not that I mind them, but the zoo has more kids than animals most days.

"No ankle biters. It'll be a chill evening checking out the zoo animals while sipping a frosty drink. It's going to be amazing."

I roll my eyes behind my sunglasses. Whatever she says. We're nearing the entrance. Vegetation lines the other side of the fence around the property so that you can't get a free peek inside. Not that you'd see animals, anyway. It's more likely to be the workers and the backs of the animal habitats.

We pass the fancy souvenir shop guarded over by giant metal statues of a giraffe family, and then Stevie points to the admission gate where Emmy and Jude wait. "There they are."

My gut clenches when I see Jude's wide smile for Stevie.

"Hey!" Stevie hugs Emmy and—I almost choke—kisses Jude

on the cheek. He looks disgustingly happy about it, too. I know she's been texting with both of them, but how much is about disc dog club stuff and how much . . . isn't? I say hello to them, but I don't kiss or hug Emmy. The last thing I want to do is to give her the wrong impression.

Stevie already has electronic tickets for all of us. I'd offered to pay for mine, but she'd declined. She holds her phone out for the gate attendant and a few minutes later we're standing in front of the lion exhibit, a frosty beer in each of our hands.

It is different visiting the zoo without kids or families around. I haven't been here in years, but I remember dodging small humans who did their best to trip you up while also waiting patiently as crowds of moms, dads, grandparents, and kids pushed strollers, dragged wagons, chased escapers, and comforted criers, all while forcing their way to the fronts of the exhibits so the kids could see better.

Don't get me wrong, I like kids and personally believe they should get all the front row viewing they want. But they make the zoo more chaotic, louder, and less desirable to visit on a normal day. Tonight is different. Small groups of adults move from exhibit to exhibit, chatting at a normal decibel level.

Take the lions, for example. Normally, wide eyes and sticky palms would be pressed against the glass to see them better. Now, a handful of people stand back so we all can gawk at the lions, hyenas, and wild dogs that share the big cat exhibit.

Unfortunately, there isn't a lot to see right now. One lone female sits on a small hill in the middle of the dirt filled enclosure. The late afternoon sun glints off her golden fur, washing her out and somehow putting a spotlight on her at the same time. She gazes imperiously through the glass at us. Intruders, her expression seems to say. Unimportant ones.

I wonder how quickly she could chase me down if she was hungry enough. Too quickly to survive, I'm sure. She tosses her head and looks another direction as if she knows she's being watched. She's magnificent.

I'm wondering if lions eat birds, and if so, which kinds, when someone touches my arm. "Logan?"

I blink and focus on Emmy.

"Ready?"

Jude and Stevie have already walked away, totally focused on each other. Emmy waited for me. She really is a nice girl.

"Sorry, I guess I was lost in thought. That lion is amazing."

"She really is. Although my personal favorites are the seals and sea lions. They're so playful."

"What about Jude?" My eyes are on his back ahead as we follow them onto the main path. "What does he want to see?" I'm not just talking about animals.

"I think he likes the tigers best."

Tigers, huh? That figures. The tiger's stalking my girl. My eyes narrow.

Emmy goes on. "Stevie said you're a big fan of birds?"

I wince. "She told you that, huh?"

Her forehead wrinkles. "Shouldn't she have?"

I sigh. "No, it's fine. It's only that bird watching isn't, you know, all that popular."

"I think it's great to have a hobby, no matter what it is."

I smile. "Thanks. I agree."

We pass a building that houses the new stingray exhibit on the left, or so the sign outside says, and I spot zebras coming up on the right. Huge, overhanging trees, low music playing through speakers hidden in rocks, free-roaming peacocks, and even the ever-present smell of animal poo adds to the zoo vibe. I relax a little. I'm here now; might as well enjoy it.

"How was the rest of your week?" I ask. "Do anything fun?"

I'd seen her two days ago at club, but we need something to talk about. She tells me about a series she's watching on Netflix about a woman who journeys alone into Colorado to build a homestead in the 1800s. It sounds good, but about halfway through her description of the show, I lose my focus.

Jude has his hand on Stevie's back. Her *lower* back, right

where it meets her butt, a place where hands really aren't supposed to visit unless they know that particular back very well. My jaw tightens, and I feel my hands forming fists. He guides her around a knot of people blocking the path but leaves his hand there for way too long after he's accomplished that goal.

When I glance back at Emmy, she's stopped talking. Her mouth twitches, and her right eyebrow is raised. "Logan . . . can I ask you something?"

"Sure." I try to focus, but half my brain is on Jude's hand. Or, more accurately, on Stevie's butt. "What's up?"

She hesitates, but then asks in a firm voice, "Are you and Stevie really just friends?"

I blink. "Yes. I mean, well, no. We live together. But if you mean are we in another kind of relationship . . ."

Words jumble and pile up in my brain. I can't quite spit out the answer to her question. We're walking past the zebras now. I feel their black eyes on me, along with Emmy's, and I start to sweat. Somewhere in the trees overhanging the path, a bird laughs at me. That's how it sounds, anyway. I finally force the words out.

"No. We're not."

Emmy nods and adjusts the strap of her small purse across her summer top. "I hope I'm not sticking my nose too far into your business here, but that seemed hard for you to answer."

I close my eyes for a second. It was hard. Way too hard. I grit my teeth, unsure what to say, and then I deflate and nod. "Yeah."

My eyes are on the zebras again. I won't say more, but it doesn't seem like I need to. Emmy seems to get what I'm not saying.

"So, here's the thing," she says. "Stevie is your best friend. Jude is mine. I've known him since college, and we're close. We don't live together like you two, but . . ." She wrinkles her nose, and her face flushes. "I wish we did. I . . . wish we were a lot more than friends."

"Oh." I straighten, surprised. "Okay." I think about it. "So . . . we might be in a similar situation."

She waits, as if she thinks I'll say more, but I can't make myself do it. I've never talked about my feelings for Stevie so openly, and especially not with someone I'd recently met. It's not easy.

Stevie and Jude stopped to check out the giraffes. They stand close beside each other at the railing. We stop farther back.

"I've been afraid to tell Jude how I feel," Emmy says.

I nod. "Same here."

"All right. We have a problem. I wonder if we can work together to solve it."

When our friends move on, we follow. We're almost to the tiger exhibit now. A metal structure that marks the edge of the enclosure has the words *Are you being watched?* on it, which draws my eyes up to a ramp above it. A tiger lies there over our heads.

"Whoa, look." I show Emmy. The striking beast looks around for a second, then lays on its side, reminding me of Bean.

The tiger habitat is circular with ramps and steps attached to the fencing for the three tigers inside to climb to the second level and move around above the visitors. A good-sized area in the middle has toys, rocks and tree trunks lying on their sides, upright climbing poles, and pools of water for the three tigers to cool off in.

Emmy sips her beer, then asks, "Is Stevie interested in Jude?"

We glance at our friends. They've made their way to the front of the enclosure standing shoulder to shoulder again. They watch as a second tiger leaps easily from one step along the fence to the next until it's also on the second level ramp. The third tiger sniffs one of the thick wooden poles, which has a ball hanging off a hook near the top.

I exhale, letting my eyes close for a second. "Most of the time, I'm not sure what Stevie wants. I'm not sure *Stevie* knows what she wants. But . . . she has seemed jazzed about Jude lately."

And I also get the sense she wants to pair *us* up for some reason. But the question is: what should we do about it?"

"Well, what we *should* do is talk to them. Tell them how we feel."

I shake my head. "I know Stevie. That would scare her away. It's too direct."

Emmy sighs. "I don't think Jude's ready to hear this from me yet, either. All right, then we'll have to get more creative. We'll talk. Come up with a plan. Okay, partner?"

"Okay." On a whim, I hold out my hand, and Emmy takes it. We don't exactly shake, more like squeeze.

Stevie turns to look for us. She sees Emmy and me sort of holding hands, and her face goes through a weird transition. First, a little shocked, then resigned, then she smiles. After a second, Jude looks back too.

I let go of Emmy's hand and lower my voice. "They're watching us."

She laughs and leans in closer. "Good. Let them wonder about us. But we'll get them to see the truth—that we're the ones for them."

"I hope you're right."

And maybe she is. Maybe this could work. Maybe, together, Emmy and I can convince Stevie and Jude they've been sniffing up the wrong trees all these years.

But as I watch the third tiger claw into the hunk of raw meat, I know it's equally as possible we'll make a giant hash of this and our friends won't ever speak to us again.

But if that happens, so be it. Something has to give with Stevie and me.

If Emmy and I can help each other, it's worth a shot.

Chapter Thirteen

Stevie

"This show is getting more ridiculous by the episode," I pronounce before carefully setting a glass of lemon water on the coffee table and flopping onto the couch.

As part of my Get-My-Crap-Together-Before-I'm-30 efforts, I've been trying to drink less wine and more water. It's working . . . some days.

Bean lies on her side on her dog bed. She shifts in her sleep, woofing a little, probably dreaming of chasing chickens again. Or discs now, I hope.

Logan nods from his spot on the other side of the couch, but I can tell he hasn't been listening or even properly paying attention to the show for the last half hour. I decide to test my theory.

Keeping my voice casual, I add, "I mean, that circus freak going berserk and stomping all over the evidence at the crime scene before saddling that rhino and riding it away was a stupid plot point, right?"

He nods again. "Huh? Yeah, yeah it was."

Like I thought. Totally not paying attention. We're watching a comedy with no circus freaks, rhinos, or even crime scenes in sight.

"Who are you texting over there?" I crane my head that way.

His phone drops into his lap in a hurry, screen down, and his cheek muscle twitches. "Emmy."

My heart spasms uncomfortably, which is weird because this is good news. News I've been waiting for.

"She was saying she had a good time at the zoo," Logan says after a minute. "Who knew adult night would be fun?"

"*I* did," I say a little peevishly.

"That's true. And it was a great idea." He smiles at me, and my heart thumps strangely again.

Logan's smile is perfect. Not only is it straight and white— *that's clean living for you*, he'd say whenever someone commented on it—but he has faint dimples that show when he gives you a real smile. I used to tease him about them, but secretly, I've always loved them.

Emmy probably loves his dimples, too. And I'm sure he loves everything about her. She's beautifully designed with her petite frame, long, shiny hair, and soulful eyes. And she's sweet and kind and a good friend to Jude. She's a patient trainer of dogs and humans alike, and she seems to like Logan, which shows her good judgment.

They're becoming friends, maybe even more, given the hand she put on his chest at the zoo. Which is what I was hoping would happen when I planned the zoo trip.

Sooo . . . why am I not happier about it? Bean conveniently wakes herself with a loud fart right at that moment, reminding me that she needs to go out. "C'mon, girl, time for bed."

Logan checks his watch. "Bed? So early?"

"Yep. It's time to tackle number four on my bucket list."

"Maintain a healthy work-life balance?"

I sigh. It's sad that Logan knows that thing as well as I do. "I've been trying to go to bed at the same time every night and wake up at the same time every morning. And no working past midnight."

He nods. "That's a good start."

If you can stick to it, his careful expression seems to say. I can stick to it. I'll show him. No, I'll show myself. This is about me, after all. Making good choices for myself and doing things I've always wanted to do.

I stand. "Want to jog tomorrow after work? We can check on the graylag and see if his mate is back. Or her mate. The mate."

Logan fidgets with his phone. "Oh sorry . . . I can't tomorrow. Emmy and I are meeting for a drink."

"Oh. Oh, well, okay. Bean, looks like it's you and me on goose patrol, girl."

She hops off the couch, tail wagging. I can always count on her. What am I saying? I can always count on Logan, too. Always. He's had girlfriends before, and we've stayed best friends. Why would Emmy be any different?

"Well, good night." Spontaneously, I lean down to hug him.

Logan stiffens. Hugs are not our normal nighttime routine, but he doesn't pull away. In fact, after a slight hesitation, he pulls me into his body. Heat flashes between us.

When I say heat, I mean flames rush from my knees, up my inner thighs, and into my stomach. The sensation singes my lungs and licks my throat. I might as well have fallen into a burning ring of fire like Johnny Cash. Or a pool of molten lava. Or something equally hot but a lot more pleasant.

For a second, I think Logan might kiss me. Do I want him to? Do I not want him to?

Confusion sweeps through me. I live with this man. We've spent hours and hours a week together since we were kids. I know him as well as I know the contours of my own belly button or the feel of the breath moving in and out of my body. And yet I've never felt this way when hugging him before.

With a rush of equal parts relief and sorrow, I step away. Logan's arms stay around me for a second, then drop. When our eyes meet, I see something in his gaze. Something . . . hungry . . . that only adds to the confusion. I turn away.

"Goodnight." I choke the word out.

Calling to Bean, I hurry to the kitchen, throw open the door, and step outside with her, grateful for the refreshing Colorado evening air. Taking deep, full breaths to calm my racing pulse, I pace around as she does her business.

What *was* that? And how do I feel about it? Thoughts, feelings, questions, emotions roll through me as I walk back and forth across the small patio. I don't dare walk outside of the pool of light on the patio and into the dark yard. I haven't picked up poop in a while.

Bean finishes up and sits by the door, waiting for me. From Rosa's yard, I can hear the soft rustling and occasional cluck from the chicken coop. I need to go to the bathroom myself after my lemon water, but I'm waiting for Logan to go to bed first. I can't face him again tonight after . . . whatever that was.

When a safe amount of time passes, I inch the back door open and listen. The living room is dark, and no sounds come from the rest of the house. I rush to my room, Bean hot on my heels, and dive into bed fully clothed.

I can't remember the last time I felt so flustered. Well, every day I feel *some* level of discombobulation but this—this was something else. It was mind boggling. Body boggling, too.

Bean paws the sheets beside me to make a nest in the empty spot on my bed, then, when she has it the way she wants it, turns in a circle three times and curls up. I wonder if she's confused, too. Usually I'd be at my desk trying to finish that one last thing that would take me until three in the morning.

Not tonight, damn it. I turn on my side, close my eyes, and will myself to fall asleep.

An hour and a half later, I'm still wide awake. I can't forget the feeling of Logan's arms around me, my ear pressed to his chest, the steady beat of his heart filling my head.

And I can't take lying here anymore, either. Time for a cup of herbal tea. Sometimes it works to help me get sleepy. Sometimes it makes me have to pee again. But I can't lie in bed fully awake a second longer.

I pad into the kitchen and stop. A light in the living room is on, and Logan sits on the couch, head in his hands.

"Are you okay?" I whisper. I'm not sure who I'm worried about waking, other than Bean. But it's too late and too dark to use a normal voice. I perch beside him on the couch.

He raises his head and looks at me. Quickly and fleetingly, red hot desire flares in his eyes. But it snuffs out quickly, making me wonder if I imagined it.

He jams the heels of his palms into his eye sockets. "I'm okay. What about you? Can't sleep?"

"No. I thought I'd make some tea. Want some?"

He nods. "Yeah, sure. Thanks."

I put the kettle on in the kitchen and then zip to my room to throw on a thick sweatshirt. It's not cold in the house, but I feel like I need a layer of protection. When the tea finishes brewing, I bring the two mugs back to the couch. Logan's upright now, but not looking at his phone or the TV. He's sitting in the dark. I sink beside him again and hand him a mug. We sip in silence.

Normally, our silences are friendly, comfortable. Not this one. It feels awkward, like we've been arguing and haven't yet cleared the air. I don't like it.

After a few minutes, I work up the courage to speak. "Logan, is everything okay? Between us, I mean?"

He doesn't speak, doesn't look at me. Finally, he sags.

"Everything's fine, Stevie."

But I have the horrible feeling that isn't true. We aren't fine. Something has shifted and changed between Logan and me, and I have no idea what.

Or how to fix it.

Chapter Fourteen

Logan

I don't see Stevie the morning after she asked if we were okay. Just as well, because I don't trust what I'd say or do. I'm totally sleep deprived and feel like I'm walking through fog. I've been kicking myself all night for not taking the opportunity she offered to tell her how I feel about her now. But I'm also not sure telling her would lead to the result I want, either.

Hoping and fearing that Stevie might come out of her room, I let Bean out to the backyard and throw the frisbee for her while I drink my coffee. When she starts nosing around the fence between our backyard and Rosa's, the disc distracts her, and she loses interest in the seductive clucking from next door.

After, I leave Bean inside and head to work, but it's a crap day. I can't focus. I can't think. I want to hold Stevie again, to feel her soft hair against my chest, and listen to her even breathing as she falls asleep. Preferably in my bed or hers, but the couch will do.

Argh, this is torture. *Torture.* Like fingernail pulling, bottom of the feet burning, guts stretching agony. I really wanted to grab her, kiss her, and tell her I love her last night, but I was too, well, chicken.

Stevie and Bean are gone when I get home from work, but there are signs she was here all day. The kitchen is kind of a wreck. I don't think number six on the list, keeping the house clean and organized, is going Stevie's way so far. But I couldn't care less.

My best friend's disorganization and messiness is part of her creative charm. She's a free spirit, and I love that about her. Along with almost everything else.

I eat some leftover pork and rice and meet Emmy at the Fiction Beer Company, a small brewery and taproom on Colfax Avenue. The place is open, bright, and cheery, and as good a place as any for romantic plotting.

Emmy and I had texted last night to make a plan to meet for a drink, a drink over which we agreed to brainstorm ways to make sure Jude and Stevie see that we're the right people for them.

"We have a problem," Emmy says as soon as I sit down at the outdoor table. Her hair's in a ponytail, she's wearing yoga pants and a cropped tank top with a pink sweater thing over it, and she has a half-drunk beer in front of her.

After the day I've had, I'd hoped for my own beer before we started talking treason, but I guess I'm out of luck. "What happened?'

"Jude asked Stevie out."

I was lounging back in my chair, but I sit up straight at that. "Damn. I knew it. I knew he was into her."

"He asked her to dinner, and she suggested going to an art gallery or something before."

"Sounds like Stevie."

Now that I'm paying attention, I see that Emmy's eyes are red-rimmed and her face looks blotchy, like she's been crying. I touch her hand. "I'm sorry. I know this must hurt. Doesn't feel great for me, either."

Truth be told, Stevie wouldn't agree to go out with someone she didn't have at least a speck of interest in. Which means she has a speck of interest in Jude. Fantastic.

On the other hand, I'm not giving her a chance to choose me. I was mute last night when I could have shared my feelings. But I can't quite commit to the idea of telling Stevie I love her and want to be with her. It feels too direct. She'll panic.

The waitress comes by and I order a Madame Psychosis, their current IPA brew, then lean forward, arms folded on the table.

"We need a plan," I say.

"I have a few ideas." She smiles, but it looks forced.

"What are you thinking?"

"We both have something, a secret weapon, that we can use." She leans forward, too. "We know them as well as we know ourselves. Example. Jude has some definite dislikes in women he dates. I'm sure it's the same with the men Stevie goes out with. If we mislead them a bit, suggest those very same things for their date with each other, maybe we can buy ourselves some time to figure out the best way to convince them we're the ones for them."

I shift my cocktail napkin around. It's not exactly mature, but it could buy time, like she said. "Okay. How?"

"First things first. Let's do this, and then we'll work on a plan for making them see reason." She sips her beer.

"What are some things that Jude doesn't like?"

"Makeup. He's not crazy about heavily made up women."

I squint. "Stevie doesn't wear a lot of makeup. I'm not sure she owns much makeup."

Emmy shakes her head slightly. "Don't underestimate the power of suggestion . . . or the depth of a woman's cosmetic drawer. If you hint that she'd look better with a full face of makeup, I'll bet she'll at least wear more than she normally would on the date."

I have no idea how to tell Stevie that in a casual way, but Emmy's already moving on.

"Now what's something that Stevie hates?" she asks.

I tell her my idea.

Emmy grins slyly. "Okay, I'll suggest that to Jude."

"Perfect. Go team." I raise a hand for her to high-five, and she pats it lightly.

"Go team."

"We've got this," I say.

And I really hope I'm right.

Chapter Fifteen

Stevie

Somehow, despite the fact that we share a less than two thousand-square-foot home, I manage to avoid Logan for the next five days. I make excuses, hide in my room, go over to Mom's house, to Tamara and Dean's, or over to one of my handful of friends' homes.

He doesn't seem to mind . . . or even to notice. Which makes me feel worse.

After he'd denied that anything was wrong, which was clearly untrue, I'd slept fitfully, wondering what I'd done to mess up our friendship. It had to be me, something I've done.

Actually, it probably *is* me. *I'm* what's wrong. I mean, who would want to continue to live and be friends with such an epic train wreck? Logan is a fully functioning adult. I can't get my life together beyond the basics of working to collect a meager income and maintaining a minimal level of personal hygiene. And I even fail at that, given that daily flossing is on my bucket list.

So, when Jude asked me out on Monday, I said yes. It was . . .

a balm for my sore ego. Someone thinks I'm okay, although I'm sure he'll change his mind when he gets to know me better.

Now it's Friday, and I'm meeting Jude in an hour, and I'm having second thoughts. I'm not in the right mood to start a new relationship. Dating is so exhausting, and it never seems to work out.

But . . . we are going to a nice place for dinner and to an exhibit at Think, one of my favorite art galleries in RiNo, the River North neighborhood of Denver, a fun and funky area chock full of old warehouses converted into hip restaurants, bars, shops, and galleries. And I like Jude, so there's that.

I take a last look at myself. I'm wearing my black summer dress, my one pair of heels, a long braided necklace, some stacked bracelets, and a few swipes of mascara and lip gloss.

I creak open my bedroom door and peek out. No sound from the living room or kitchen, so I tiptoe to the back door to let Bean out before I go. I haven't told Logan I'm going out with Jude, and I'd as soon avoid the teasing he'll undoubtedly inflict on me. He always manages to find something to criticize about the guys I go out with, and the longer I go out with them, the worse it gets.

No luck in sneaking out today. Logan's leaning against the kitchen counter, drinking from a bottle of water and looking at his phone. He glances at me, and I straighten my shoulders.

"Hey. You look nice. Where are you headed?" He sounds distracted. Uninterested.

"I'm meeting someone at Think."

"Yeah? Who?" He looks at his phone.

I sigh. "Jude."

He nods and sips his water. "Cool. Have fun."

Frowning, I step outside with Bean, hoping to close the door and end the conversation, but Logan wanders out.

"What are you doing tonight?" I ask him.

"Going out with Emmy."

He is? Since when? I knew they'd been talking, but this is

new. And I'm glad about it. Right? Number one is happening like I planned.

"Oh. Where are you going?" I ask.

"We haven't decided yet. Dinner. Then we'll see."

O-kay. Hello, vague. "Well, have a good time."

"Thanks, you too. Oh, and Stevie—a tip," he says in a bored voice. "You might want to put on a little more makeup. Emmy told me that Jude likes women who look really polished. I guess he dated a makeup artist a while ago and he got a taste for it. Or something like that."

I stare at him. How weird. But I guess he's trying to help. "Thanks."

I leave Logan outside to put food in Bean's bowl and order my Lyft to go downtown. Then, I glance at my watch. I have a few minutes.

I dart to my bathroom and add more blush. And more lipstick. I layer on the mascara and try to add some eyeliner which frankly doesn't go very well. Finally, I use this contouring stick that Tamara gave me, so my cheekbones are more defined, and I brush a finishing powder over my face with a tiny bit of glitter in it. The final impression is kind of . . . overdone, in my opinion. But it's definitely more *polished* than before.

Logan's walking to his room as I leave. He looks my way, and his eyes widen. For a second I wonder if he's about to laugh, but his face immediately calms.

"Looks great," he says. "He'll love it. Have fun."

I leave, feeling more confused about my friend than ever. As I ride in the back of the Lyft, the driver talking my ear off about the upcoming presidential election, Jude texts that he's waiting outside the gallery and looking forward to seeing me. How sweet.

As I step out of the car, I catch a reflected look at myself in the rearview mirror and nearly stumble. Clearly, my bathroom mirror isn't as bright as daylight. I don't look polished; I look like a poorly drawn clown.

But I'm out of options because Jude's right here. I turn my look of horror to a smile and greet him. His warm expression slips when he gets a good look at me, and his eyes go wide like Logan's had.

"Um, hey," he says, "you look . . . great."

"You too."

And he does look good, but ugh, he *smells* terrible as he leans in to kiss me on the cheek. Like he threw a canvas bag over my head and squirted lime juice and alcohol directly into my nostrils. He's never worn cologne before. Why now? I hate fragrances. They make my eyes water, and I always . . .

"Ah-choo!" I double over.

Oh boy, and now I need a tissue. I dig one out of my bag and blow my nose. Jude and I stare at each other. He looks scared, and I back away a step to avoid a second wave of nasal assault.

I groan inside. Why didn't I trust my own instincts about my makeup instead of listening to Logan? I'm no cosmetics expert; I never wear much. I shouldn't have tried to lay it on thick with two minutes to spare in a dimly lit bathroom.

What the heck's wrong with my best friend? From his shocked expression, Jude clearly *doesn't* like a heavily made up woman. And if there's one thing I am tonight, it's that. With a forced smile and holding my breath to avoid sucking in more of that awful fake citrusy scent, I follow Jude inside to make the best of it.

We stroll around Think for about an hour, checking out the pieces on display. The current theme is community. The art is mixed media with photography, which is my favorite, and the works include paintings, sculpture, and illustrations of things you'd find in a community, which can really mean anything. There's even a little room with an experimental auditory and olfactory piece that replicates the sounds and smells of a garbage truck rumbling through an urban neighborhood. Which somehow still smells better than Jude.

I'm apparently as eye-catching as the art. More than one

visitor to the gallery does a double take as they pass me. Eventually, I can't take it anymore. Before we leave for dinner, I excuse myself to the bathroom to wash my face. It takes two and half rounds with industrial hand soap and paper towels, but I finally get the whole mess off. Luckily, I find an old tube of clumpy mascara and a lip gloss in my bag, which I apply after using hand cream on my poor skin. Now I'm kind of ruddy red, but it's better than before.

Jude smiles a genuine smile—of relief, I'm sure—when he sees me. "Um, I hope you aren't offended by this, but you look so much better without all that makeup. Beautiful, in fact."

"Thanks." I smile back and then add on a whim, "I only wore so much because Logan told me that Emmy told him that you appreciate women who look really polished, including lots of makeup."

His eyebrows pinch. "She did? Really? I don't know why she'd say that. I'm pretty sure I've never said that. Ever."

"Huh." We start walking. The restaurant is a few blocks away.

"So . . . let me ask you this," he says. "Do you *adore* cologne?"

I squint at him apologetically. "No, not really."

"I was wondering. Emmy said Logan told her you did."

I almost choke. "Um, no. It's the opposite of true."

His mouth quirks. "Sorry about the way I smell, then."

"I've gotten used to it. I try to picture you swimming in a gin and tonic." I wink at him.

We're laughing as we arrive at Il Posto, a posh Italian eatery down the street from Think. The hostess seats us at one of their high-backed round booths. We talk about the art for a while, then about work, and finally the conversation comes around to the club.

"Are you and Bean signing up for the Colorado Canine Challenge?"

I finger my glass of rosé. "Do you think we're ready?"

"For the novice division? Absolutely. She's a natural, and your throws have come a long way."

I snort. "Thanks. They had a long way to go." A few of my first ones hit the dirt so fast it was like they were being shot at. "Are you and Emmy going with Meadow?"

"They're competing in the advanced division for distance and Meadow and I are in freestyle."

"I can't see how either of you will lose. You're amazing."

He runs a hand over his jaw, which has the perfect amount of stubble, in my opinion. "Meadow's the amazing one. I guess we're good at helping her show her skills, but—"

He doesn't finish his sentence, because without warning, Emmy and Logan pop out from around the side of the curved booth.

"Surprise!" Emmy says. "We're making this evening a double date."

She slides in next to Jude, and Logan sits beside me. He doesn't look as excited as she does. As for Jude and me, I'm pretty sure the waiter could walk naked out of the kitchen and we wouldn't be as surprised.

"How did you know where we were?" I ask.

"Jude told me," Emmy says.

"How . . . fun." I'm not sure what else is appropriate to say.

My date's eyes narrow at Emmy, but when he looks at me, I nod to let him know it's okay with me if they stay. Logan sighs.

"We haven't ordered yet, so you aren't far behind if you want to join us," Jude says grudgingly.

"Great!" Emmy scans the menu.

She cleans up well. She's wearing an adorable floral halter mini-dress and heels, her hair is super-straight and sleek, and she's wearing the perfect amount of makeup. My own face is still raw from the scrubbing. But that wasn't her fault. I don't think.

"You look great, Emmy," I say.

"Thanks, you too! Love your dress."

I sneak a peek at Logan. He's focusing on the menu like it

might hold the secret to everlasting happiness. I realize I'm glad to see him. A double date *is* fun, even if we didn't pre-arrange it. On the other hand, I'm suspicious. Why did he tell me Jude liked women to wear a lot of makeup? What are he and Emmy up to?

Whatever it is, we don't talk about it. The conversation floats from the upcoming competition, to politics, to the latest blockbuster movie that none of us have seen but agree we should, and ends with us enthusiastically noshing our food, including a divine flan for dessert.

When it's time to go, Logan and I decide it makes the most sense to share a Lyft home. Jude kisses my cheek again before I get in the car. Not exactly the most romantic of goodbyes, but Logan and Emmy were standing there waiting for us.

"What was that about?" I ask Logan in the car. Although I'm sure the Lyft driver doesn't give a crap what we're talking about, I keep my voice down.

"What was what about?"

"The double date. The makeup thing. The cologne thing."

He glances sharply at me. "I mean, the double date was Emmy's idea. Otherwise, I have no idea what you're talking about."

I glare at him. "I think you do. Jude definitely does *not* like a lot of makeup. And you know I hate cologne."

"I didn't force Jude to douse himself in Old Spice." He snickers.

I huff. "It wasn't Old Spice." Frankly, Old Spice would have been better than whatever Jude had worn.

"So, good date?" Logan asks.

"Best one in a long time. Jude's a really nice guy." I turn to the window, so I can't be sure, but I think the smirk slides right off his face.

Good.

I don't know what he thinks he's doing, but whatever it is, I'm not playing along.

Chapter Sixteen

Stevie

The morning of Bean's first competition blooms like a bright, beautiful wildflower. The sky is a pale blue, showcasing the dandelion yellow sun, and the grassy park where the Colorado Canine Challenge is being held is a vivid green thanks to some rain the last day or two.

The Denver Disc Dogs club members, me included, are gathered together under a couple of tents near the competition field, and Bean is living up to the caffeinated variety of her name. She can't sit still, constantly moving at the end of her leash. She watches the groups of dogs and humans as if she would love to herd each and every one.

"Looks like she's excited." Jude nods toward Bean.

He's especially cute today in a tight-fitting shirt and jeans. His dark hair is getting longish. I think about curling a lock around my finger, but I abort mission at the last minute, when I feel Logan's eyes on us. Why does he seem to be watching me so much lately? Especially with Emmy here?

"I'm going to warm Bean up," I tell Jude.

I can't quite put Logan and our problems out of my head as I dig in my bag for one of the discs I brought. It's been really awkward between us since the unplanned double date. And I can't exactly avoid him all the time. At least he seems to be spending more time with Emmy, who really is great.

Our captain is already warming up, throwing the disc for Meadow. The border collie is doing her dead-level best to show the competition they have no chance. Which they probably don't. I watch them for a moment, marveling at how athletic Meadow is, how smooth and even Emmy's throws are, and what a great, in-sync team they make.

I sigh. Bean and I are nowhere near their level. But that's what novice means, and at least we're here, she's super excited, and the club has checked off items seven and three on my list: *learn to do something new* and *travel somewhere new*. I've never been to this particular park in Littleton. It might be stretching things a bit to call a suburb of Denver a "new" place, but I'm allowing it. Hey, it's my list, after all.

Bean and I find some space among the human and dog teams. "Ready to train, Beanie Weenie?"

I start by throwing the disc a few times at short distances to focus her. I've found she does better when I give her a chance to warm up and adjust to the activity. I try to keep a similar warm up routine every time, even using the same words before we get started so she knows what's in store for her. She gets treats after she retrieves the first few throws to reinforce the behavior, and I keep the warmup easy. She needs to save her best sprints and catches for the actual competition.

The youth division will compete first, then the novices, and finally, the stars: the advanced catch and throw group and the freestylers. Emmy will team with Meadow for the advanced group and Jude will partner with her for the freestyle.

Bean only has me, poor thing. My throws still tend to go a little wild, but she's patient with me. And at least she's having fun. She practically grins every time she brings the disc back to me. We're working on commands like drop, and I'm trying to teach her to recognize a signal of when to start running by pulling the disc behind my back before throwing it. I forget sometimes and she doesn't listen or pay attention other times, but we're starting to get the hang of it.

"Stevie!" Logan calls my name. "Stevie, over here!"

I crane around to see him. Logan stands beside a very familiar couple. The guy has dark, wavy hair that brushes the tops of his shoulders, and she's slim, blonde, and has a wide smile. I wave, leash Bean, and walk over to say hello.

"Travis! Amelia! I didn't know you'd be here," I say.

"We're the official mobile veterinary clinic for the competition," Travis says with a wink before hugging me. "Hey, Bean, how are you, girl?"

Bean dances in a circle on her back feet. She *loves* both Doctor Travis, her vet, and Amelia, his fiancée and assistant. Like, almost as much as me or Logan.

That might have to do with the fact that she's never needed any real veterinary treatment outside of her puppy shots and regular exams, or it might be that they keep a steady supply of treats nearby when they do see her, so she's associated them with a yum factor. It could also be that they'll swing through Park Hill to visit her when they can, so every time she sees them isn't associated with something sharp, scary, or otherwise off-putting.

Whatever their magic sauce is, I wish I had some. She barks excitedly and darts a few times around their legs. Travis laughs and tries to slow her down long enough to pet her.

"How's the wedding planning going?" I ask. "I got the save the date notice for December. I'm so incredibly happy for you two!"

"Thank you!" Amelia answers. "It's been a ton of work to plan on top of trying to grow the practice, but we can't wait any longer."

Travis and Amelia have been engaged forever. Or at least it feels that way. They're finally tying the knot at a fancy dude ranch

THE CONUNDRUM OF COLLIES

owned by one of their clients, and I can't wait to go. I've already booked a room at the ranch as a Christmas gift to myself. They had a cheaper lodging option, but this seemed like a great way to relax and celebrate the holiday season. I got double beds and mentioned the weekend to Logan—he knows Amelia and Travis, too, thanks to their visits to the house. But now . . . I'm not so sure.

"Expand the practice?" Logan asks.

Travis nods and tries to thrust his hands in his pockets before apparently remembering he's wearing scrubs that don't have them. He laughs and crosses his arms.

"Yeah, we're so busy, we're starting to have to refer new patients, so we're thinking about buying a second RV and hiring another vet and assistant team to join the practice."

"Where is the Love & Pet mobile?" Logan glances around. "Never mind, I found it."

The RV is hard to miss. Parked over in a side lot, the clinic on wheels is an eye-popping shade of turquoise blue with the Love & Pets Animal Clinic logo on the side. I'm proud to say I designed the logo for Travis and his grandma Jo a few years ago when they started the practice. They were my clients first, and now Bean and I are his. I even went to Jo's funeral when she passed away soon after Travis and Amelia met.

"How are you two?" Amelia asks Logan and me.

"Yeah, good." I avoid Logan's eyes. He doesn't say anything at all.

When I twitch and smile awkwardly at Amelia, her own happy expression slips. She glances between Logan and me, but thankfully she doesn't say anything.

"What brings you two here?" Travis asks from beside Bean. She's on her back now, legs splayed for a belly rub.

"Competing," I say. "This is Bean's first."

Travis's eyes go wide. "I didn't know Bean was a disc dog."

"She is as of this summer," I say. "We joined a local club, and we've been getting great instruction." When I look to Logan for confirmation, he looks annoyed. But why? Emmy is an amazing teacher.

"That's wonderful!" Amelia says.

Travis agrees. "Bean will do great. High energy border collies are perfect for this sport."

"She does seem to love it, although we're still working on the basics. If you want to watch, we're in the novice group. Our start time is supposed to be around ten." I check my watch. "And I'm running out of warm up time, so I better go."

I hug them again, and they give Bean final pats on her back. I smile tentatively at Logan before going to find Emmy and Jude. I need to focus on getting Bean ready.

"Hey." Jude grabs my hand when I walk up. "Who was that?"

"Bean's veterinarian. You have to meet Travis and Amelia. They're amazing with animals and such a sweet couple. They're getting married at a ranch in December. Hey, maybe you can come with me!" My voice hitches at the end, when I remember that if Jude is my plus one, Logan can't be.

"Sounds great," Jude says.

Ugh. I've accidentally invited Jude to a wedding that's still months away. Even though I've only known him for like a month. And I've already mentioned it to Logan.

Normally, I'd feel confident my friend would understand, but these days, it seems less likely. As Jude leans down to scratch Bean's side, I close my eyes for a second and breathe.

I'll have to sort this out later. Somehow.

Chapter Seventeen

Logan

Yeah. I officially hate this.

As I watch Jude and Stevie holding hands and talking, inches apart, I know, deep in my thirty-year-old bones, that it should be *my* hand she's holding and me she's looking to for support.

After saying goodbye to Amelia and Travis, I trudge back to the club's tent home base. Aaron and Nisha sit in camp chairs chatting. Aaron and Bear are competing later in the advanced division. It's their first time, he'd told me earlier. Nisha and Jack came out for moral support. Their dogs hang out in a foldable metal pen set up for the canine crowd.

Everyone gets ready to watch as the youth competition gets underway. I pull up an empty chair beside the others, but my eyes can't stop finding Stevie and Jude standing close together as they watch the kids and dogs step to the line. Emmy puts Meadow in the pen and sits beside me.

She lowers her voice. "Hey, you okay? You look sort of . . . thunderous."

"Thunderous?"

She smiles sympathetically. "Like a thunder cloud. Like you

might start yelling or pound on someone soon." Her gaze follows mine. "I hope you don't pound on Jude."

My shoulders slump. "Nah, pounding isn't my style. But I'm not happy about how things are going."

"Me either."

We'd agreed that the surprise double date last weekend might not have been the best idea. Not only had heavy makeup and overdoing the cologne not deterred Stevie and Jude, they were both annoyed with us for showing up unannounced, which in hindsight we probably should have anticipated.

Stevie had seen Jude at least twice since then, Emmy told me, and worse, she seems determined to avoid me, too. It's been almost a week, and I've barely seen her, except for at club on Wednesday, where everyone was focused on getting ready for today.

Emmy told me that Jude had as good a time with Stevie as she did with him. Which means our initial plan failed utterly. Emmy and I watch our friends for a minute. They're standing even closer, if that's possible, and smiling foolishly at each other.

"We'll figure this out." She pats my arm and speaks to the group. "Not many kids are competing. If we want to watch the novices, we should grab spots closer to the field."

Emmy, Aaron, Nisha, and I along with Chloe, Scott, and a few other folks from the club carry our chairs to the edge of the competition area, a rectangle with boundaries marked and distances measured with chalk lines across the grass. Tall orange cones support ropes and flags that outline the perimeter.

The first competitor in the novice division steps up, a guy with a white and brown, meaty pit bull. From what I've seen so far, border collies like Bean and Meadow, Australian shepherds, or some mix of the two, are the most common types of dogs here. I've also seen breeds like whippets, Labrador retrievers, and cattle dogs.

"Are pit bulls common?" I ask Aaron.

"I've seen a few," he says. "But this one doesn't look too focused."

The pittie's owner uses treats to try to keep his dog's attention, but the dog looks totally overexcited. He's running in circles, chasing his tail, his tongue hanging out of his mouth. Maybe it's the crowd, the other dogs, or the pumping music they've been playing, but the poor guy is focused on everything except the purple disc his human futilely waves in his face.

Nisha shakes her head and laughs. "This isn't going anywhere good."

Sure enough, when the guy lines up and throws the disc, the dog bolts away . . . in the wrong direction. He's apparently spotted a hot canine specimen behind his human, and he's sniffing her butt instead of chasing down the disc. The frisbee lands yards away in the grass while the guy has to retrieve his pit bull.

"Beginner nerves," Emmy says.

"Hopefully Bean's not watching," Jude says as he sits on Emmy's other side. "They're up third."

After a few more unsuccessful attempts to capture the pit bull's attention, the guy gives up. He shrugs dramatically for the crowd and leashes his dog. Everyone laughs and claps for his heroic efforts.

The second contestant is a thin middle-aged woman wearing long shorts and a wide brimmed visor. Her canine partner is a mostly white Aussie with black patches over the eyes and some freckles on the body. This dog seems more prepared. Most dogs, even the experienced ones, dance around excitedly, as if they pick up on the crowd's energy and know they're performing. This one stands calmly in front of her handler, keeping an eye on the blue disc she holds. The woman throws, and the Aussie takes off. The throw isn't terribly long, and the dog catches it with ease.

"Hmm, they're good for newbies," Jude says.

The Aussie brings the disc back and drops it at the woman's

feet. She throws a second disc, longer this time. The dog still catches it with ease.

"Uh oh, they're looking good," Aaron says. "I smell a winner."

Nisha smacks him on the arm. "Don't say that. Stevie and Bean haven't even gone yet."

He raises an eyebrow. "If these two don't make a mistake on their last throws, Stevie and Bean may not *need* to go."

In a competition, pairs get sixty seconds to complete as many throws and catches as they can at distances up to about fifty yards. The longer the throw, the more points the team gets, and they're awarded a bonus half point if the dog leaves the ground completely to catch the disc. Meadow does this with ease; Bean . . . not so much. But she's new to it. catching the thing and bringing it back is a major accomplishment at the novice level.

Stevie has trained Bean using a stopwatch, trying to get her doing as many runs as she can in the time allotted. She usually averages about three or four. This lady and her dog are going to make it to five throws.

Aaron's right. This pair will be hard to beat. But then, on the last throw, a breeze suddenly picks up, lifting the disc erratically at the end of the flight arc. The Aussie was running at a pace well-timed to catch the disc until it jumps, but she misses it, and the frisbee falls to the ground.

A groan of disappointment rises from the watching crowd, followed by applause for the pair. The woman waves in acknowledgement and rubs her dog affectionately when it returns with the disc.

A minute later, Stevie and Bean step to the line. I can tell right away Stevie's anxious. She's not terribly tall to begin with, but she seems to shrivel a little when she's nervous. She pushes her wavy hair behind her ears and licks her lips. Then she leans down and whispers to Bean.

Bean looks nervy, too. Instead of standing steady, like the Aussie had, she's hopping around Stevie. High energy isn't necessarily a bad thing, I guess, since she's about to take off running, but she also looks distracted. Not as bad as the pit bull, but still.

"C'mon, Beanie Weenie, you've got this," I mutter.

Nisha snorts and leans around Aaron to grin at me. "Beanie Weenie?"

I shrug. "That's Stevie's nickname for her."

Nisha chants. "Bean-ie Ween-ie, Bean-ie Ween-ie!"

The others pick up the chant, and Stevie looks over, flustered but smiling. The timer must start because she jerks, turns, and throws the disc.

It's a shortish throw to start, something Emmy told Stevie to do so that Bean has a successful initial catch. Which she does. We all cheer, and confidence seems to infuse Stevie. She stands straighter and puts her shoulders back. Bean brings the disc back and miraculously drops it at Stevie's feet. Stevie throws a second disc about twenty-five yards. Bean catches it easily.

She returns it, and Stevie throws a third time, the longest one yet, thirty-five yards. Bean leaves a little late, but she's totally focused on the bright yellow disc.

It looks like second place is imminent until Bean stretches out long and snatches the disc before it hits the ground. The crowd cheers loudly, which distracts her a bit, and her return to Stevie is slow. They might have time for one more throw.

In a rush, Stevie botches the fourth throw. It's unbalanced, and the wind catches it, making it not as long as her previous try. Bean sets out at a sprint, then has to adjust her pace. In the last second, she twists, and with all four paws off the ground, snatches it out of the air. The club goes wild, cheering and clapping for them.

"That has to be first place," Jude says.

He jumps up and jogs over to Stevie to wrap her in his arms. I stiffen and grit my teeth. It's like knives under my fingernails to watch Stevie turn to Jude, her face lit up with pride and joy. Almost as bad is watching Bean jumping up on Stevie, then on Jude. When my friend comes over, I congratulate her quietly.

Stevie sits on the far side of Jude, her legs tucked up in front of her and nibbling a thumb nail, as we all watch the next few novice teams go. Each pair comes close to Stevie and Bean's score, but they don't quite beat it. The dogs lose focus, the wind takes the disc off course, or the teams are too slow.

I slump in my chair, thoroughly defeated. Why am I even here? I'm happy for Stevie and Bean, but Stevie obviously doesn't care about my support. As each team goes, I get increasingly ticked off. She seems to be actively ignoring me, talking to Emmy and Jude. If this is how she's going to play things, then this will be my last club event. It's her and Bean's thing, anyway. I came with them to spend time with Stevie.

When the novice group finally finishes up, and the runner ups are announced, I find myself spitefully hoping Stevie gets second.

But she doesn't. She and Bean take first. She jumps up, hopping up and down like a denim and Converse clad frog, and hugs Bean, then Jude, then Emmy.

I smile, glad for her despite myself. And then, completely unexpectedly, she runs to me and leaps in my arms.

"We did it, Logan! We won!"

Shocked, I catch her and hold her tight. I don't know if I'll get this chance again, so I'm going to savor every last second.

Chapter Eighteen

Logan

I'd had high hopes after Stevie jumped on me like that after she and Bean won. But they'd been crushed like a beetle under a car tire. Another week had gone by, a week of Stevie spending all her free time with Jude and encouraging me to see Emmy.

I'm stymied. It's time to bring in the voice of experience. I need advice—family style.

Friday after work, while Stevie is out with Jude, I take Bean and her disc over to Tamara and Dean's house for a clandestine visit. Jazzy meets me at the door.

"Uncle Logan!" She's called me Uncle Logan ever since Dean jokingly referred to me like that a year or so ago. I give her a hug before releasing her so she can smother Bean with kisses and hugs.

"Want to throw Bean's frisbee for her?" I ask. "She needs to practice."

Jazzy's eyes light up. "Yeah!"

I hand her the disc and she and Bean tear out the back door to the yard. Stevie told me that the Escape Artist had gotten out of their yard before by pushing a weak fence lock open with her nose. Dean fixed the lock, but I'll keep an eye on them just in case.

Tamara beckons me into the kitchen. Soft music plays through a portable speaker, and something that smells delicious bubbles on the stove.

"Grab a beer or glass of wine or whatever you'd like from the fridge. Your text sounded like you need one."

I extract a beer from behind leftover containers and perch on a barstool at the two-person island. Dean wanders in from the hallway that leads to their bedrooms, his hair wet. He shakes my hand and gets his own beer.

"Need help, hon?" he asks Tamara.

"No, we're almost ready here. It's pasta, grilled chicken, and a salad, Logan."

"Sounds perfect; I'm starving," I answer. "When are you two headed back to school?"

"In two weeks for our teacher workdays. The kids come back a week after that." Tamara sighs. "I love my kiddos and my coworkers, but the end of summer is always bittersweet."

"We're trying to decide on one more blowout Adventure Thursday for next week," Dean says. "Any ideas?"

I shake my head. "You've already done everything I could possibly think of. You may have to repeat. What was last week's?"

"We hiked Pyramid Peak near Aspen," Dean answers. "It's a class three fourteener, so it was a challenge."

"A challenge?" Tamara snorts from the sink, where she's draining the pasta. "It almost killed us."

"A challenge, like I said." Dean winks at me.

Fourteeners are fourteen-thousand-foot mountains that are categorized into five classes. Class one peaks aren't easy, but they're at least hike-able. Class threes involve areas of scrambling over rocks or unroped technical climbing. Class five requires full technical climbing.

"Have you done a class four or five yet?" I ask.

"Not yet. Maybe next summer," Dean answers.

"Not ever," Tamara plops a dish of pasta down in front of us and narrows her eyes at her husband. "We have a child, remember?"

"I'll work on her," Dean mutters as his wife walks away.

"You can try," she says over her shoulder.

Tamara recruits us to move the food to the small dining room.

"I hoped we could eat outside," Tamara says, "but we're supposed to have some storms this evening." Thunder booms almost as soon as the words come out of her mouth, and she lifts a hand as if to say *See?* then walks to the back door, probably to call Jazzy in. She needn't have bothered, Jazzy and Bean scurry through the door before she can say a word.

Jazzy clutches her mom's leg, and Bean comes to me, ears down and tail between her legs.

"That was scary, Mommy," Jazzy says. "The sky got really dark and the clouds were *mad.*"

Tamara hugs her. "You're safe now. Time for dinner; go wash up."

Tam's food, even the simple stuff, is always delicious, but I don't enjoy eating it as much as I usually do. Dean had asked where Stevie was tonight and thinking about it gave me a cramp.

Eating with Jude. Smiling at Jude. Kissing Jude? I can't think about if she's doing any more than that with Jude. Considering her kissing him is already more than I can stand.

I guess I don't hide my mood very well, because Tamara touches me on the shoulder as I wash the dishes after the meal and asks, "You okay, Logan? You seem a little . . . down."

Dean's bathing Jazzy and putting her to bed, and Stevie's sister dries the dishes as I wash them. It's as safe a time as any to unload on her. With a few pauses to clear my throat and paw around inside myself to get at my real feelings, I tell her what's been happening the last couple of months.

Tamara listens quietly, the towel in her hand moving methodically around dishes as I pass them to her. "Okay, so Stevie's working through her thirtieth birthday bucket list, and she's seeing a new guy. But . . . why does that bother you?"

Enter extra pauses, more pawing, and a few awkward stammers. "Because, you know, I always thought that by the time we were this age, we'd be, well . . . together."

"So, you're saying you want that to happen now?"

I nod and take a deep breath. Time for the truth to come out. "I love Stevie, Tam. I think I've always known that, but I was willing to wait and let things develop. Except they aren't developing. She either doesn't feel the same way about me or she's fighting it. And I don't know what to do about it."

Tamara squeals and hugs me so hard I almost drop a soapy glass into the sink. "Oh, I was hoping you'd say that. Dean and I have been betting on this for years with Carol and my dad."

I must look shocked, because she pats me and laughs. "I'm sorry, I know nothing's settled yet. But everyone's going to be so excited if this actually happens." She grins again, but then settles her expression, and her voice is gentle when she asks, "Have you tried telling Stevie how you feel?"

"No," I groan. "Things have been so weird between us. Like, we get along well, but this is the elephant in the room for me. I can't pretend I don't have these feelings for her anymore. I don't know if she feels the change, but I think she might because she's been avoiding me and spending every spare minute with Jude the last few weeks." I can't help biting off his name.

Tamara lays out the last few things to dry on the towel-covered counter, and we move to the living room. Outside, the rain is coming down hard and lightning fractures the dark sky every few minutes. Bean, who sat between my feet while I washed up, now shadows my every step. She's terrified of thunderstorms. Tamara and I settle onto the couch, and I pet Bean's head after she curls up against my leg.

"So," I say, "has Stevie ever mentioned how she feels about me?"

Tamara shakes her head. "I mean, we all know she loves you. But does she *love* you, love you?"

"That's the question, right?" I run a hand through my hair. "I'm tired of being friends. I want more. But every time I try to show that, Stevie backs away. I'm afraid if I have a real, adult conversation with her about this, that she'll freak out."

Tamara tucks her legs under her and pulls a fleece blanket over them from the back of the couch. "I understand. But don't you wonder if Stevie might be worried about the same things? I know she isn't one to really express her feelings—"

I grunt. Understatement.

"So maybe she's running away to avoid facing the same things you're worried will happen. Logan, I've known you almost as long as I've known Stevie. You are right for her, and I think she's right for you. But I don't know many couples who get together without actually talking about it first. I mean, you could sweep her into your arms and kiss her passionately and admit your fiery love for her, but with Stevie?" She shakes her head and rolls her eyes. "You're liable to find her halfway to Canada."

"I agree. So, what do I do?"

Dean comes in then and grabs another beer from the fridge. "Do about what?"

Tamara sighs as he sits in a lumpy overstuffed chair, looking expectant. "Okay, quick recap. Logan loves Stevie and wants her to know it, and quickly. But she's dating some other guy right now and seems to want Logan to hang out with another girl. Got it?"

The beer floats inches from Dean's mouth. "Damn. When did all this happen?"

She waves impatiently at him. "While you were putting the baby to bed."

"And over the last thirty years," I add.

"Right," Dean says. "Glad I got a six-pack. This is clearly a two-beer conversation."

Over the course of the next hour, we come up with and

discard about ten ideas for how to approach the problem of Stevie.

"The girl is too stubborn for her own good," her sister laments.

"Or I'm completely unappealing," I say.

Tamara pats my hand and jokes, "You're not *that* unappealing, Logan."

"You know what you need?" Dean's finishing beer two and tapping his fingers against the arm of the chair. "Something that gets her out of her comfort zone. Catches her off guard. Shocks her. Maybe if she's a little off balance, not so defensive, she'll be able to hear what you're saying."

"Like what?" Tamara asks.

An idea pops into my head. "I've got it. Number two on her bucket list."

Dean leans forward. "What's number two?"

"Skydiving."

This could work. I can set it up, go with her, and when she's good and petrified that she might die, tell her I love her.

Tamara claps excitedly. "Yes! And . . . it's the perfect Adventure Thursday."

Chapter Nineteen

Stevie

Thursday morning, I pack a backpack and Bean and I head outside to wait for Mom to pick me up. Logan was up and out early this morning, probably for a coffee meeting or something. I hid in my room until he was gone, even though he took longer than usual to actually get out the door.

After winning the novice division at the Colorado Canine Challenge, I'd been riding high. I couldn't believe Bean did so well. And we weren't the only ones who'd had a good day.

Emmy and Meadow, and then Jude and Meadow, had won the advanced and freestyle divisions, and Aaron and Bear came in third in advanced. The club had a rare sweep of the main events, which made the day super exciting for everyone . . . except Logan. I'd babbled all the way home about all the wins, but he'd been very quiet. I could tell he was happy for me, but after my initial excitement, we went back to being awkward. Which hurt and confused me.

And then there's Jude. I've seen him several times this week, and I do like him, but he seems to want to take things faster than me. I'm starting to have the feelings of doubt that always creep in after a while when I get to know a new guy. He's too this, or not enough that, and I'm not sure he's quite right.

But . . . the clock is ticking. Not my body clock. I hate that expression. Plenty of women a lot older than me marry and have children. I mean that my birthday is in two weeks, and I'm starting to wonder if I'm being too darn picky. Jude really is sweet . . . and there's daunting item ten on my list.

I'm supposed to be falling in love with someone. Why did I put that on there? Because I'd been twenty-five at the time and assumed it would be easy by the time I was thirty. Stupid Stevie.

Mom swings into the driveway a few minutes late and harried as usual. She's already talking before I even get the door open.

"So sorry, Stevie Sunshine. I could not get out of bed this morning. I was up late working on a contract, and you know I need at least seven hours."

"I know. It's okay." I kiss her cheek. "I'm sure Tam and Dean won't mind. Do you know where they're going? They didn't tell me."

It's their last Adventure Thursday of the summer, so I assume it will be something extravagant. I'm planning to take Jazzy to the museum, and then out back to the park to play in the fountain and eat a picnic lunch.

"No, I have no idea." Mom answers quickly. A little *too* quickly.

I glance at her. Why in the world wouldn't she tell me where they were going if she knew? I have no idea. I don't know much these days.

We pull into the driveway, and I get out, then stop, head tilted. Logan's car is here. I look at Mom and point at it with a questioning expression.

She shrugs, but a way-too-innocent expression takes over her face. "I have no idea why he's here, hon. Let's go in and find out."

Inside, the living room is mysteriously empty. Tamara, Dean, Jazzy, and Logan are nowhere to be seen. I walk toward the kitchen with Bean trailing and almost have a stroke when they all pop up from behind the kitchen island.

"Surprise!"

I grab my chest and step back. "What the heck is going on? What are you doing here, Logan? Surprise for what?"

"It's your birthday, Aunt Stevie! But I want to go on Adventure Thursday, too." She whines the last part and grabs her dad, peering up at him hopefully.

Dean groans. "We've told you, Jazzy. They wouldn't let you. You're too young and you don't weigh enough. And even if you weren't either of those, Mom and I wouldn't be comfortable letting you skydive yet."

I gasp. "We're going skydiving?"

Tamara swats her husband. "Dean, you ruined it." She turns to me, shaking her head. "Surprise! We're taking you skydiving for your birthday. Mom's babysitting Jazzy and Bean. We're all going, and Logan already paid for your dive, so you can't back out."

I cover my mouth and gasp. "Oh, thank you! But it's so expensive. Are you sure?" My eyes find Logan.

He smiles his familiar smile, and the warmth I see there reassures me. He wants to do this. For me. For my bucket list birthday. What an amazing friend he is. I hug him, holding on longer than I probably should. When I pull back, everyone is staring. I move away quickly.

"What do I need?" I say.

"To get in the car!" Tamara says. "We have to get up to Longmont. Our safety training starts in an hour and a half."

I kiss Bean on the head and hug Mom and Jazzy. "Thank you!"

"You're welcome," Mom says. "Have fun and oh, Logan, get that video that you said the company will take. Don't forget! Lamar and Jazzy and I want to see it!"

"You got it," Logan says, winking at Mom and high fiving a

still pouting Jazzy. "Ready?" When he holds out his hand hesitantly to me, I take it.

"This is so incredible," I say. "Thank you!"

"You're welcome." He squeezes, and I squeeze back, and I feel a surge of love for him. He's my best friend, no matter what. This has been a hiccup. Relationships have them.

Outside, Tamara and Dean throw a bag into the back of their minivan and argue about which route to take to the Longmont airfield, so we have a private second or two.

I study my friend. "What's on your bucket list, Logan? I've never asked."

He smiles softly and helps me into the back of the van. "I'll tell you one of these days."

"Taking I-25 to the Longmont exit is best, love, like they said on the website," Dean says from behind the wheel as we get on the road.

"No, babe, if we want to avoid traffic, we should go toward Boulder and take 287 up and then over to Longmont," Tamara argues.

"You guys have the sweetest arguments," I say.

"Best way to stay married." Dean says to me in the mirror. "Don't worry, you'll see."

I snort. "Sure about that? I'm no closer to finding a husband than I was at Jazzy's age."

Dean guffaws, and Tamara smacks his arm again, harder this time. She shoots him a warning look, although I'm not at all sure what he's done wrong. Logan looks out the window.

The ride to Longmont takes a little over an hour. We get there in time to use the restroom, grab a drink of water, and report to the briefing room. The safety video takes about half an hour, and then we're introduced to our instructors. We each have our own, because we're doing tandem jumps. Mine is Seth, a burly, bearded, tattooed guy, and Logan has a wiry older man named Mike.

Tamara and Dean meet their instructors, and together, we

decide that they'll dive first, so we can watch them for a minute or two, and then Logan and I will go. Supposedly, we'll all land near each other. I hope.

"Here." Logan hands me my hoodie and jacket out of his backpack. "I brought you these. They said it can be cold at 18,000 feet, even in summer." He hands me my layers, and our fingers brush together. His eyes warm again. "Excited? Number two on your list is nearly in the bag."

"I'm *so* excited. And so touched. Thank you for planning this."

Something flares in his eyes . . . an intensity . . . like he wants to say something important, but he turns away, patting the front pocket of his jeans as if reassuring himself something is there.

My nerves kick in around the time we're fitted for jumpsuits and Seth shows me our shared parachute rigging. He assures me he's already checked it thoroughly. He'll wear it and engage it when it's time. I'm responsible for me and my borrowed safety goggles. But that makes me more anxious, in a way. I have zero control of this situation. I excuse myself to use the restroom one more time.

When I come out, Logan's talking to our instructors. I wouldn't have noticed anything weird about the interaction, except that they all smile, Seth shakes his hand, and Mike pats him on the shoulder, then they clam up as soon as they see me. Odd.

"Ready?" Logan asks me.

"Scared to death, actually," I say. "But ready as I'll ever be."

He puts an arm around me and hugs me to him. "You've wanted to do this forever. You've got this."

I nod and smile at him, grateful that he's his normal self today. I've missed him, I realize. Missed our easy friendship. I squeeze his side, then Tamara, Dean, Logan, and I follow the instructors and the videographer Logan is paying extra to film my jump into the twin engine, jet-prop airplane. The propellers spin, making a whole lot of noise, and the smell of fuel makes me hold my breath.

The flight up is uneventful . . . if you call being petrified about the possibility of free falling for hundreds of feet while hoping a large piece of fabric will keep you from slamming into the ground at one hundred miles per hour uneventful.

And then we're at jumping altitude, or whatever the video called it. Most of the thoughtful, thorough safety training dribbled out of my head on the way up here, along with any sense of security I usually possess. Terror takes its place when the instructors tell us it's time.

Dean high fives me from his seat on the other side of Tamara, and my sister hugs me.

"Happy thirtieth birthday, Stevie. I hope this is your best year ever." She glances at Logan, and her eyes sparkle in a mischievous way. His face gives nothing away.

We stand so the instructors can attach the tandem harnesses to each of us, and then Logan and I hold on to metal grips on the sides of the airplane and watch as first Tamara, brave soul, and then Dean jump with their instructors. Tam half screams and half laughs as she falls out of the side of the plane, and Dean hoots as he goes.

I need to pee—again.

"We're up, Stevie," Seth says from behind me. I realize in a vague way that he's completely calm and confident despite my abject terror. Or probably because of it. "But Logan has something he wants to give you before we jump."

We're already attached through the harness, so I have trouble peering around at Logan to see what Seth could possibly mean. Did I mishear him?

Logan swims into view beside me, hands me a folded piece of paper, and kisses me—full on the lips. I don't have time to ask him what he's doing, or even to think, because Seth hustles me up to the open door. The videographer jumps out first, ready to film us.

The wind rushing by almost rips the paper from my hand, but I have a moment to open and read the note, written in Logan's neat print, before Seth hauls himself and me into the rushing, ethereal, glittering blue sky.

My already pounding heart and sweaty palms hit overdrive. Because, to my absolute astonishment, the note that's now crumpled in my fist says:

I've loved you since I met you, Stevie Watson.
Be mine.

Chapter Twenty

Logan

I don't know that much about skydiving, but I'm convinced that this is the longest free-fall in history. Or maybe it only feels that way.

Mike and I cut through the air like tethered asteroids. My stomach stays somewhere overhead as the wind rushes past my ears. The ground grows alarmingly nearer and more detailed with every passing second. Not to be overly dramatic, but I feel closer to dying than I ever have, with the possible exception of when my bike brakes went out on a steep hill one time in my teens.

I'm not ready to die.

I want to really kiss Stevie. I want to make love to her. I want her by my side as we go through life, and now, I've pretty much told her so.

As I'm starting to wonder how much farther we'll fall and if something's gone wrong with the parachute, Mike deploys the canopy. With a startling jerk, we stop falling and start floating. I take a long breath and try to relax.

Now that I can focus on something other than impending death, I check out the view. The Rocky Mountains spread to the west and the wheat-brown high plains to the east, the skyscrapers of downtown Denver stand to the south. The clouds feel close enough to stroke their fluffy surfaces, and I wouldn't be surprised to see a bird lazily wing by at eye level.

"Doing okay?" Mike asks from behind me.

I give him two thumbs up. If I hadn't just laid my heart in Stevie's hand in the form of a scrawled-on slip of paper, I'd be perfect. But as we get closer and closer to the landing area, reality sets in.

Stevie had read the note, glanced at me with wide eyes, and dove out of the plane with Seth. I'd watched her fall with fear like a stick of dynamite in my gut. Not the fear of us dying in a horrible skydiving accident. The fear of rejection.

How will she react? Will she be happy about my surprise admission or angry or disappointed or regretful? What will she say?

Despite the certainty of my own feelings, doubt sets in, and a clamminess crawls up my spine. Maybe this wasn't a good idea. Stevie's a free spirit, but she doesn't always appreciate surprises. Then again, my feelings would have been a surprise no matter how I shared them with her. I had to tell her how I felt. At least this way she gets a little time and space to think about how to respond.

I watch as the videographer, and then Stevie and Seth, land smoothly in the grassy field below, running a little ahead of the parachute. Within a few minutes, Mike and I are on the ground, jogging ahead as our own canopy collapses softly behind us.

Tamara and Dean and their instructors are already unharnessed with their parachutes collected. As Stevie, Seth, Mike and I collect ours, my anxiety grows. Stevie hasn't even looked my way.

"Mike, thank you. That was fantastic," I say. "Once in a lifetime experience."

He shakes my hand. "You did great. But it doesn't have to be once in a lifetime. You guys are welcome back any time." He grins and tilts his head toward Stevie, who's walking with Tam and Dean to the van waiting to take us back to the hangar. "Maybe for your honeymoon?"

I grin. "We'll see."

I'd felt like I should tell the instructors my plan earlier, so they'd know what I was doing when I handed Stevie the note. I'd asked if they were okay with it.

"Depends on what she says," Seth had said with a laugh.

And now, as Mike and I join the others at the van, it's the moment of truth. What will Stevie say?

When she throws her arms around me to hug me, my body melts and my heart busts into frenetic, excited thumping. She loves me. She wants me, too. Maybe she was even waiting for me to admit how I felt. She knew all al—

"Thank you so much for the incredible birthday present, Logan," she says. "That was worth waiting thirty years for." She's smiling, and she's looking at me, but she's not quite meeting my gaze, if you know what I mean. Her eyes slide away immediately.

Oh, crap. Not good. Not good at all.

She's referring to the skydiving, not my note. If she wants to be with me too, she'd say so now. If she needs more time, I think she'd still acknowledged the note. But her reaction, a genuine but careful thank you for my gift, is the worst possible response. It means, I think, that she's buying time to decide what to say. Or to pretend my note—my admission of true freaking love—didn't happen.

With a growing sense of doom, I follow her toward the van. She sits beside me in the second row and talks excitedly over her shoulder with Tamara and Dean about the dive. They respond, obviously having loved it too, while simultaneously shooting anxious, worried glances at me. I try to pull myself together.

It's not easy.

I have to share the back of the minivan with Stevie on the way back to Denver as she goes on about how amazing it all was. She can't wait to see the video, which they'll send in a few days after editing, and she's so excited she can check the experience off her bucket list.

She apparently loved everything about today except for me offering her my heart.

"Lunch anyone?" Dean says when we get back into Denver. "We have Carol for a few more hours."

"Oh, I can't," Stevie answers. She doesn't look my way, but I can tell she's making an excuse about needing to get home to work on a project.

As for me, I need to get out of this van and somewhere away from Stevie. Her hair, her glowing skin, the animation in her voice, even her slightly salty scent are conspiring to send me tumbling into a deep chasm of self-pity that I can see myself never crawling out of.

Holding Jazzy's hand, Carol runs out to the driveway as we pull in, her expression worried. "Stevie, Bean escaped from the backyard again! Jazzy and I went inside for a few minutes to get lunch and left her outside, and when we checked a minute ago, she was gone."

Stevie groans and hands her bag to her sister. "Can I borrow some turkey?"

"Turkey?" Tam shakes her head and blinks.

"To catch her with."

"Yeah, of course, can we help?"

"No, I've got it." Stevie says this with a resigned voice.

"Logan will help. Won't you, hon?" Carol says to me.

I look from her, to Tamara and Dean, whose expressions are suddenly full of understanding and compassion, and finally to Stevie. Who won't meet my eyes.

I scoop up my bag and shake my head. "I'm sorry. I'm . . . I have to go."

Head down, I hurry to my car, get in, and drive away. Like a coward. But you know what? For once in her life, Stevie will have to deal with her own mess.

Without me.

Chapter Twenty-One

Stevie

Mom, Tam, Dean and I watch, open-mouthed, as Logan speeds away in his car.

"Why did he leave so fast?" Jazzy looks as puzzled as everyone else.

I think I'm the only one who can answer her question, but then I see Tam's face. My sister studies me, concern lining her face, and I realize she knows about the note. Or at least about the feelings that Logan expressed inside.

I look away. I can't talk to her about this right now; I have to track down Bean. I reach for Jazzy's hand.

"C'mon, I think I know where Bean went," I tell her.

I can feel, more than hear, Mom and Tamara exchanging quiet words behind my back. I wonder what Tam tells her. Whatever it is, I'm sure I'll get an earful about it later.

In the kitchen, Jazzy and I fish out some turkey from the fridge to put in a baggy. I lead my niece out the back gate and in the direction of the house where I found my dog the last time she ran away.

I can't believe Bean did this—again. I really thought the disc dogs club was helping her outgrow the desire to chase chickens. She hadn't been over to harass Rosa's flock in weeks. Why now?

While we walk, Jazzy chatters away about a game that she and Mom played. It involved some form of hide and seek crossed with the hot and cold game, where Jazzy would hide a doll and then yell from her hiding spot whether Mom was getting closer or farther from it as she moved around the house. Jazz didn't understand how Mom found *her* so easily every time after locating the doll.

As we approach the hen house, she suddenly asks, "Aunt Stevie, why didn't Uncle Logan stay and help?"

I squeeze her hand. "He probably had some work to do. Or he had to be somewhere else."

She thinks about that, tilting her head. "But . . . he didn't hug me. He always hugs me before he goes."

My heart contracts. "That's true. He must have forgotten. I'm sure he will next time." I pet her curly hair. "He'll be okay. I promise."

Why did I avoid saying anything to Logan about the note when we landed from the dive? I'm sure that's what he's been wondering, and he's drawn his own conclusions. But honestly, *I* don't even know how I feel. I was floored when I read his words, and between my shock and the free fall, I didn't have the time or brain space to think about how to respond.

Knowing how he really feels about me is exciting, frightening, and unsettling all at once. My insides tangled right up like a pot of overcooked noodles. If I'm honest with myself, I guess I'd suspected his feelings about me had . . . shifted. He'd been hanging out with me a lot more over the last year or two, not dating as much, and more recently, he's seemed weirdly hostile toward Jude. I'd tried to put a little distance between us, thinking it would reinforce our friend boundaries, but that hadn't seemed to work.

And now this. I'm sure he wanted me to run into his arms when we landed from the jump and tell him I felt the exact same way about him, but honestly, what did he expect? His gesture was grand, romantic, and completely out of character for him. I was blindsided. And now that he's come clean, I'm terrified that if I say anything but that I love him back, I'll lose him forever.

My hand comes away sticky from my niece's hair. Stuck *to* something, actually. An apple green lollypop—stick and all. I try to pull the candy around so she can see it. "Uh, Jazzy? Did you lose something?"

"Oh! There's my lollypop! I couldn't find it." She tugs it out of her hair, yelping a bit when some strands come with it, peels the hairs off, and pops it in her mouth again.

Yuck. Kids. But I love her.

We're at the house now, and I can hear the clucking fowls. I'm no backyard bird expert, but they don't sound particularly distressed. I trot to the fence and look in. There's no sign of Bean. I call for her. Nothing.

The same older woman, wearing the same worn robe as before, pokes her head out the back door. She must recognize me, because her face contorts into a frown. "Lost your beastly dog again?"

I squint apologetically. "I thought she might have come here. Have you seen her?"

She shakes her head. "No." She thrusts a broom through the door and shakes it. "But I'll use this on her if I do. I protect my flock!"

"Okay, thanks anyway." I take Jazzy's hand again, and we hurry back toward the house. This is not good. Bean isn't really a runner. She usually stays in our yard or visits Rosa's flock. Could she have been taken? She is a pretty dog. My heart thumps unevenly and sweat makes my shirt prickly.

Jazzy's anxious questions turn teary. "Why was that woman so mean? Where's Bean? Where did she go? Do you think she's okay? Why did she run away?"

"I don't know, Jazz, but she can't have gone very far."

We check as many backyards between the hen house and

Tamara and Dean's home as we can but find no sign of Bean. She hasn't come back to my sister's house, either. Mom walks out of the kitchen with Bean's collar in hand.

"Wait, she's not wearing her collar?" Nails of panic shoot into my brain.

"She rolled in something stinky in the backyard," Mom explains, "so I took her collar off to wash it."

I take the damp strap of nylon from her. "Can you take me home, please? I need to see if she went there. If not, I'll get on my bike and ride around to look for her."

"Of course," my mother says. "And I'll drive around for as long as I can after dropping you off. I have an appointment, but I have some time to look for her."

"I'll keep looking here too," Dean says.

"I'll help, Daddy!" Jazzy says.

"Thanks, nugget." He kisses her head, then sniffs it. "Why does your hair smell like apple?"

Mom and I gather our stuff and head for the car. Once buckled up, she keeps throwing me anxious looks. Although I'm turned toward the window, searching yards, sidewalks, and alleys along the way for a slim, glossy haired black and white beauty, I can see my mother's worried reflection in the glass.

"Stevie, what happened with—"

"Mom, please don't ask. Logan and I had . . . a disagreement. That's all. We'll be fine."

She nods but doesn't look convinced. "He's never left like that, when you needed him. And he looked upset."

"I know, I know. I'll talk to him. Except I need to find Bean first."

Mom is quiet. Let's hope she stays that way. My tension grows the closer we get to home. Will Bean be there? Will Logan be there? What *will* I say to him? No, I can't think about him right now. It's bad enough wondering if I'll ever see Bean again.

If I don't find her in the next half-hour, I'll email the neighborhood watch and friends I know between here and there to be on the lookout for her, and I'll call the animal shelter and the Denver Dumb Friends League. At least she's microchipped. Someone will find her, right? Please let someone find her.

Logan's car isn't there when we get to the house. Mom pulls in the driveway and lays a hand on my leg. "Let's find Bean first, but then please call me. We need to talk."

I glance sharply at her. She has her mom face on, the one that means she isn't playing around. She's got something to say, and I'm going to listen. Wonderful. I nod and hop out. "Thanks for helping with Bean."

"Of course, Stevie. We'll find her."

Please, please let that be true. If I lose Bean *and* Logan . . . I can't go there. Let's just say life as I know it will end. While that's probably terribly melodramatic, it's true.

I search the house, the yard, and even peek into Rosa's yard, but no Bean. No Logan, either. Where is he?

I have no time to ponder that. Instead, I extract my bike from the detached garage, pump up the tires and start riding. Up and down streets and alleys between our house and Tamara and Dean's house. I call for Bean, over and over and over.

I see lots of other dogs and their humans as I go. I stop to show them pictures of Bean and give them my number to text or call if they see her. But no calls come in.

The family is silent, too, other than periodic check-ins. Lamar texts to say he's taking up the search party when Mom has to go to her appointment. Hours go by with no good news.

Finally, at seven o'clock, I give up and go home. I'd stopped by our house a few times to check the yard, get water, and send out SOS emails. I'd called the shelter and the Dumb Friends League twice. Nothing.

Leaving the fence gate open for Bean—wishful thinking—I sink onto my bed, phone in hand but otherwise paralyzed with fear and fatigue and watch the evening shadows stalk across my Bean-less room inch by inch.

Sometime around midnight, I startle awake. There's movement in my room. Bean whines.

"Bean? Beanie? Come here girl!" I pat the bedspread blearily, wondering if I'm dreaming. If so, don't wake me.

She leaps on the bed, and I smother her with kisses and hugs, not even caring that she smells like manure and has what feels like dirt and dead grass in her fur. I tell her over and over how much I love her. And then, carrying her lest she escape again, I creep out of my room.

No lights are on, and as far as I can tell, no one is there. Not in the kitchen, the living room, or Logan's room. The back door is locked, and the yard looks undisturbed. As I'm peering out through the window in the kitchen. A car starts out front.

I hustle that way as fast as I can with a forty-pound dog in my arms. When I finally get the locked front door open, Logan's car is driving away down the street.

He'd found Bean and brought her home.

And left again without a word.

Chapter Twenty-Two

Logan

Okay, call me a complete and utter pushover; you'd be right. But I couldn't let Bean go missing without doing anything to try to find her. Or let Stevie suffer over it.

As soon as I'd driven away from Tamara and Dean's house, I'd changed my mind about leaving Stevie to deal with her own mess and gone looking for Bean. I love the dog, too, after all.

Ten hours and several texts to Dean to make sure Bean hadn't turned up later, I hadn't found her. I'd called shelters, posted in neighborhood Facebook groups, texted friends, drove around some more. Basically, I blanketed the neighborhood.

I'd known Stevie and her family would be looking too, and for some perverse reason, I'd wanted to be the one to find her. Wanted to be the hero, I guess. Maybe I wanted Stevie to owe me. I dunno.

But when I'd heard from a friend near midnight on Thursday that he'd gotten home to find Bean trapped in his yard in Park Hill somehow, I'd driven over to get her, slipped her inside the house with Stevie, and left. Another buddy had already said I could crash at his house that night. All I'd known was that I couldn't face Stevie.

And now? It's Saturday, and I still haven't faced her. She's called and left messages thanking me for delivering Bean to her, which I haven't answered, and she'd texted yesterday morning that she wanted to talk, but she needed time to think and sort out her feelings. I'd planned to stay at my buddy's house again, but Stevie surprised me by taking Bean to her parents' house for the weekend. I appreciate that she's giving me the house while she thinks this through.

I love Stevie. I want Stevie. But I'm pretty sure I can't live with Stevie anymore and just be friends. It's too painful. Either my note results in us working things out or I'm moving out. I won't tell her that unless I have to. But I've decided.

It might be difficult to understand how a grown woman like Stevie wouldn't know how she feels about me, her oldest relationship outside of her own family, but I believe her. She's always had a hard time identifying her feelings.

When we were ten, she'd dumped an entire container of granola and some milk inside Tamara's made bed after Tam ate the last of the sugary cereal Stevie had wanted.

Carol grounded her, made her vacuum up the mess, strip the bed, wash the sheets, and remake it. But when she interrogated Stevie about why she did it, Stevie simply said Tamara should have asked if anyone else wanted the Fruit Loops or whatever before she ate them. When we laughed about it years later, she told me she hadn't been angry at the time. In that moment of granola-dumping, she just really wanted those Fruit Loops. Stevie acted first and felt later, always. That time she got revenge, this time she's running away.

Understanding this about her, I'll give her time to think. Not forever, but for a while.

Saturday afternoon, right when I've run out of things to do to stay busy (clean the house, run, game, nap, examine the ragged edges of my fracturing heart), Emmy calls to ask if I'd like to come over and have dinner. I think I break speed walking records going over there.

When I arrive at her condo in the three-story brick building in City Park South, Meadow meets me at the door. I pet her and follow her inside. Emmy's place smells great, like grilled meat, and soft music plays from a speaker somewhere in the bookcase on one wall of the small, square living room.

I've never been to Emmy's place. And every time I've seen her before, she's worn normal things like summer dresses, shorts, jeans, whatever. But tonight—tonight she's dressed to stop hearts. Barefoot and in an emerald green, off the shoulder mini dress with her hair down and begging to be touched.

Except . . . not by me.

While she's sweet, kind, gorgeous, and talented with a disc and a dog, I don't have any romantic feelings toward her. I thought she knew that. But now I'm not so sure. And, to make things worse, I'm totally underdressed in my jeans and flip-flops.

"Um . . . hey." I hand her the six-pack of beer I'd brought. We'd learned quickly that Emmy's a beer drinker. No wine or cocktails for her.

"Hey, glad you could come." She leans in to kiss me on the cheek, sending bolts of alarm shooting through me. She's never kissed me before, even on the cheek.

"Thanks for inviting me. It's been a rough week."

"Yeah? Why?" She checks her watch and turns back toward the stove, where she's stirring something that smells both sweet and spicy. I bend down and pet Meadow in order to avoid staring at her mistress' backside in that dress.

I think about telling Emmy about skydiving with Stevie, but it's still too painful, and frankly, I don't know how the dive ends. I've been suspended in mid-air since Thursday. Instead, I make an excuse about work and ask how I can help her get dinner on the table instead.

She has me make a curry and mayo-based dip for some vegetables she's grilled. Then I set the table. As I do, and we talk about this and that, I wonder what it would be like to *really* fall for Emmy. Or any woman other than Stevie. My Fudgsicle-shaped heart was claimed by my best friend when we were six, and I have no idea how to free it.

As Emmy and I carry plates loaded with chicken kebabs with a peanut satay sauce and the grilled veggies and dip to her small, round dining table, I'm hit again with the realization that I'd made the right decision to tell Stevie how I feel. She needs to face her own feelings, and if they don't match mine, we need to free ourselves from the friends-but-we-could-be-more knots we've tied each other up in. I don't want to lose her, but I can't live like this.

As Emmy puts the last of the trimmings on the table, I excuse myself to use the restroom and wash my hands. When I get back, I realize she's shimmied the chairs so we're sitting less than a foot from each other.

Hesitantly, I sit beside her and lift my beer glass to toast hers while Meadow settles under the table by our feet. Her nose lifts up, sniffing the air under the food. "Thanks again for having me over."

"My pleasure." She looks at her watch again before taking a sip.

Which makes me glance at my own. Three minutes to eight o'clock. "Are you . . . waiting for something?"

"No, sorry." She touches my leg. My thigh. I'm terribly tempted to scoot my chair away from hers. Or at least ask her what the hell she's doing. "Try your kebab. The satay recipe is from my mom."

I slide a nugget of grilled chicken off the wooden stick and dip it into the sauce. It tastes as outstanding as it smells: tangy and savory with a nice touch of peanut butter. As I chew, I hear a key turn in the lock behind us and the door opening.

As Meadow shoots to the door, barking, Emmy grabs my face and kisses me. Like right on the lips. Which could have at least been enjoyable if my mouth wasn't full of chicken satay. I don't push her away or anything because I'm doing my best not to choke.

When she lets me go, I finally turn toward the open door. Jude's hand is on the door handle, and his mouth hangs open like he'd been about to speak. While Meadow jumps on him, whining, his eyes roam over Emmy. She stands with a hand on my shoulder while I swallow the mouthful and finally get to my feet.

Slowly, he tears his gaze away from Emmy's long legs and her hand that's now on my lower back to take in the dinner table, the room, and I think even tries to place the artist currently playing through the speaker.

He blinks and runs a hand through his hair nervously. "Looks like I've interrupted. Sorry, Logan. See you, Emmy." He stalks out the door, almost closing it, but then darts back inside and drops a set of keys on a side table. "Thanks for letting me borrow your car."

And he's gone.

I turn to Emmy, speechless. I thought she knew I wasn't interested. She knows how I feel about Stevie, and she loves Jude, right? Or have I fallen into some alternate reality?

Emmy's hand drops off my back, and she leans against me, laughing. "Did you see his face? If *that* doesn't make him think about how he feels about me, then I don't know what will."

I put a hand on my chair to steady myself. "You mean you were . . . this was . . . You were *pretending* because you knew he was coming over?"

Emmy's face grows contrite, but she giggles. "Yes, I'm so sorry to, well, sort of use you like this, Logan, but I knew Jude was bringing my keys back at eight and I thought it was now or never. I had to show him what he was missing out on."

"Why didn't you tell me what you were doing? You scared the hell out of me. I mean that dress, and sitting all close like that . . . I thought I was going to have make an excuse and get out of here before things went much farther."

"Honestly? I didn't think we could pull it off without

laughing or looking like we were faking it. I'm really sorry, but your shocked reaction when he came in was really genuine. And priceless."

I let out a long breath. "I wasn't shocked by him coming in. It was *you* kissing me. And almost choking."

"Forgive me, Logan. I didn't know what else to do. Nothing's working with Jude."

I shake my head and lick my lips. "No, it's okay. I'm only glad the kiss wasn't real."

She laughs, perfectly normal again, and pats my shoulder. "You're a great guy, Logan, but Jude has my heart, and I know Stevie has yours. Sit and eat. I'm going to throw on some jeans, and I'll be right back."

When Emmy returns, we eat, drink beer, feed scraps to Meadow, and I tell her about skydiving, the note, and Stevie. And she listens like a good friend does. After washing up, we take Meadow for a walk through a night-darkened City Park, and I head home.

Nothing got decided about Stevie or Jude, but it was a very good evening and—near heart attack aside—I was glad I'd gone.

Chapter Twenty-Three

Stevie

On Saturday morning I pack a bag for myself, collect up Bean's food, dishes, and her disc, and retreat to the relative comfort and safety of family.

After skydiving, the life-exploding note from Logan, and his heroic return of Bean, which I'm still not sure how he managed, Bean and I are going to spend the weekend with my parents.

Logan and I need space, I'd decided. Other than needing a bath, Bean had been fine after her own Adventure Thursday. But believing my beloved dog had been permanently lost or stolen made me nauseated, shaky, fearful, and unable to sleep. I'm so grateful to Logan for finding her and I want to thank him properly, but I need the time to think about what *else* I'm going to say. His note gave me plenty to think about.

Mom and Lamar are home when I arrive. I don't know what Tamara told them, but since I'm at their house for an impromptu sleepover, I'm pretty sure my folks can tell something's wrong. They don't pressure me to tell them what it is, bless them, instead letting me settle into the guest room.

Mom pops her head into my room a bit later. I'm sitting on

the bed with my laptop, Bean conked out on the floor. I try to keep her off the furniture when I'm here, although I'm not always successful.

"I'm going to my appointment now, and Lamar's leaving in a few minutes to meet some friends for lunch. If you're free this afternoon, I'd like to take you somewhere. Lamar's offered to make us dinner afterward. Sound okay?"

I smile and agree half-heartedly. Mom already made it clear she wants to *talk*. I wish I could avoid it, but I probably owe her an explanation after asking to flop at her house for the weekend. Everyone does so much for me, and I doubt they'd say the same in reverse.

In fact, I've been thinking about creating a whole new bucket list after my birthday, one that's focused entirely on helping and doing for other people. It seems like the perfect choice for my fourth decade of life.

Bean and I go out to the backyard when my parents leave, and I lay on a shaded lounger, alternating between scratching Bean's noggin and throwing the disc for her. I can't focus on my current project, a drawing for an old college friend who's having her first baby that I plan to give her at her shower next month. I'm not hungry, thirsty, or interested in reading or watching TV. Instead, I listlessly toss the disc, hoping to wear Bean out.

As if she can tell I'm not in the mood, she drops the disc in the grass and comes back to hop up on the lounger at my feet. She lies down between my feet and puts her head on my knee. Her amber gaze searches my face as if to ask what's wrong. Or maybe where Logan is. Or if I happen to have any bacon. Who knows what she's thinking? But my eyes well up with tears at the compassionate look on her face.

She knows something's wrong, and she wishes she could help.

When Mom touches my arm, I bolt awake, then wince. My neck is stiff. "What time is it?"

"About four. Sorry to wake you, but are you ready to go on a little trip with me? It won't take long."

I rub my eyes and smooth my tangled hair. "I'm ready. Can we take Bean? Or should I put her in the laundry room?"

"Lamar's home. He said he'd keep her inside with him and watch her."

I pull on my sneakers and go inside to thank him, calling Bean as I go. I'm probably lucky she didn't try to escape while I was napping, although I think I would have felt her jump off. She was still on the lounger when I woke up.

The truth is, I don't know if I can trust her on her own anymore, even in fenced yards. She's too prone to wandering, herding, chasing, and generally doing all the naughty things. It's hard to accept, because otherwise she's such a bright, gentle, and obedient dog. Another thing weighing on my heart today.

After I make sure Lamar and Bean are set, Mom and I head out to the car.

"Where are we going?" I ask.

She smiles mysteriously. "Not far."

I sit back and watch the familiar streets of Park Hill slip by. Not many people were born and raised *and* still live here. After five minutes, Mom pulls down a street I haven't been on in a long time and parks in front of a brick ranch style house that I know almost as well as my own. It has a Sold sign out front and the yard needs a mow. I throw Mom a questioning glance.

"C'mon." She gets out and leads me to the back.

My eyes slide over the house as we go by, the very first house I lived in. The one my mother brought me home from the hospital in as a baby. And I know the house next door about as well. That's where Logan's family lived when he and I were kids. Mom opens the fence gate.

"Are you sure this is okay?" I ask.

"The previous owners already moved out. The new owners are doing some work on the kitchen and floors before they move in, and their realtor said it would be fine if we stopped by."

We enter the yard, and I can't believe what I see.

My old swing set is still here. And when I say old, I mean *old*.

It's not one of those fancy wood structures that families have now. This is the four-legged metal style with a rickety, chain link swing, a butt-roasting metal slide, and a couple of rings that Logan liked to hang from and pretend he was a monkey.

It was here, at the foot of the slide, that we kissed and agreed to get married someday. While covered in ice cream, my scalp aching from my Mom's nit picking and Logan's hair shaved within an inch of its life after a bad case of lice. I smile at the memory before an arrow of pain pierces my chest. The pain of what to do about Logan.

Mom strolls around the perimeter of the yard, checking out rose bushes, Russian sages, and annual beds that long since passed out of her realm of responsibility. "I have good memories from this house. Not perfect, but good. This was where I brought you home after your dad left. This was where I met Lamar and fell in love. And this was where you met Logan, your very best friend."

I sit on the swing and pump my legs gently, getting it moving. I still get a bit of a head rush from swings, although not until I'm going a lot higher and faster. "I have good memories of this house, too." I finger the metal chains of the swing. They're rusted, but still strong. "You were a really good mom, you know. The best."

She gave me everything she possibly could, from love to strength to guidance to the occasional grounding when it was needed. She even found me a loving stepfather and an amazing stepsister, who has since brought a loyal brother-in-law and an adorable and fun niece into my life. They love me despite my bad traits. What more could I ask for from family?

Mom sits on the bottom of the slide. "Thank you, Stevie. That means a lot to me. I worry about you, you know."

I lick my lips nervously. "I'm fine, Mom. Really."

"I know you are. You've created a career for yourself, on your own terms, and you have good friends, including that sweet dog of yours. But I want even more for you. A dog is a wonderful companion, but you need a life partner. Someone to love and care for . . . and someone to love and care for you."

I stare at my feet as I swing. New Converse are needed; these are almost shot. I've had a series of about eight pairs of these sneakers over the last fifteen years. I'm attached to them. If I'm honest, I don't really like change. New things scare me. Maybe that's why I put off tackling my bucket list for five years.

Mom watches me fidget, and when I don't answer, she sighs. "Stevie, what's going on with Logan?"

It's my turn to let out a long breath. "We've . . . hit a rough patch."

"What kind?"

I tell her everything, haltingly. Our playful discussions about getting together over the years. Feeling things had changed between us recently. Trying to push him toward Emmy. His note. How he slipped Bean inside the other night without another word. Mom nods knowingly, like she's not even surprised.

"Why do I feel like you already know all this?" I ask suspiciously.

She wrinkles her nose. Her makeup is perfectly matte despite the warm afternoon sun. How does she do that? I've never known. Half the stuff other people do are a mystery to me.

"Well, Tamara and Dean heard from Logan that his feelings toward you had been shifting. They helped him cook up the plan to take you skydiving and give you the note. He thought it would make for a really great story, but . . ."

"I ruined it." I hang my head. I didn't handle any of this well. Not at all.

"But Stevie, it's all right if you *don't* share Logan's feelings. I know you two are very, very close, but sometimes feelings don't change from friendship to more for both people. Sometimes that's only in Hollywood, and it could even be for the best. Some friendships should stay just that. But what does Logan say? Have you spoken to him?"

My head hangs lower, and I mumble, "Not exactly. I haven't

been sure what to say."

Mom nods. "I wondered if that might be the case when you asked to come over. Well, how are you feeling about him?"

I let go of the red-brown chains and throw up my hands, almost falling back into the grass. "I don't know! I'm terrible at figuring out how I feel."

She thinks about that. "Let me ask you this, then. Picture your life a year from now. What does it look like? What's different, and what's the same?"

I answer immediately. "Everything's the same. Everything's exactly the same. Logan and I still live together with Bean."

She makes an encouraging sound. "And are you friends? Or more than that?"

I drag my feet on the ground to stop the swing. "I don't know! That's what I can't figure out. I don't want to lose what I have—or had—with Logan. And I'm so afraid I'm about to lose that, no matter what I do or say! Why did he have to do this? Why couldn't we stay the way we were?"

Tears well, and a teensy tiny connection makes its way through my brain. I was terrified of losing Bean on Thursday. And now I'm terrified of losing Logan.

Is that how I want to live? Do I want to hide from loss and avoid change? Hang on to old things because they were good once? I mean, of course I don't want to lose my dog, but pets age, they get sick, they lose abilities. And so do humans. Relationships change all the time. Jobs change. People move away.

Nothing stays the same. I know this on some level, but I can't seem to apply it to my relationship with Logan. He's always been part of my life. Always.

"You and Logan have had a connection since your days playing on this swing set," Mom says gently. "Of course, it's hard to think about that changing. When you picture your relationship changing to something more, what frightens you about it?"

I stand and pace. "Everything. Logan and I have never had a physical relationship. I mean, other than hugging or sharing a blanket on the couch once in a while. What if we aren't, you know, compatible? What if it's awful? What then? I lose him. I lose my best friend."

"Or . . . maybe it will be wonderful. At least half of a relationship, if not more, is the emotional connection. You two already have that down. And you manage a home successfully. You know each other's strengths and what you aren't so good at. I have a feeling that you'd work through anything that wasn't quite optimal in the physical department."

I stop walking. "Then you think I should say yes?"

She shakes her head. "Oh no, Stevie Sunshine. I didn't say that. That's your decision to make. I'm trying to help you work through this. I do understand your concerns, but please consider this. Life is change. The reason your relationship with Logan hasn't changed, is because you two have worked so hard to hold on to what you have. Through other romantic relationships, through career changes and shifting priorities, you've stayed together. Yes, as friends. But you've proven your relationship can withstand years of change already."

That stops me in my tracks. She's right, we have. Examples: Logan's company offered him a nice promotion a few years ago that would have required him to move out to California. He'd turned it down because we'd recently signed the lease on our house, and he didn't want to leave me to find a new housemate. I'd had a boyfriend after college who was pretty serious about wanting me to move in with him. I didn't, because it would leave Logan scrambling to find someone else to share with, and the guy and I had ended things soon after. We'd each made sacrifices to stay near the other.

I collapse on the swing seat again. "What if this is different, though? What if our friendship can't withstand being in love?"

Mom stands and takes my hands. "There's one way to find out, love. Logan has told you how he feels. The change you fear is here—whether you like it or not. Now, it's up to you to decide how it turns out."

Chapter Twenty-Four

Logan

The next few days after Stevie comes home, we move through the house like polite, quiet ghosts. Instead of best friends, we're acquaintances. Instead of housemates, we're tourists. Instead of falling in love, we're falling apart.

Monday and Tuesday, I drag myself to and from work, make quick meals in the kitchen, and spend evenings in my room instead of the living room. Stevie seems to be doing the same.

The house is a wreck, the fridge is practically empty, and my heart's frozen with grief. I want Stevie, but I don't want to lose her all together like this.

Something has to give.

Emmy texts me on Wednesday afternoon. *Coming to club tonight?*

I don't know. Don't think I'm up for it, I text back. And don't think Stevie wants me there anymore, I don't add.

Come. I have some exciting news. Please?

I heave a long sigh. I'm guessing her news has to do with Jude, and I'm happy for her, but it makes the horrible ache in my chest harder to bear. I'm having a hard time finding anything

A.G. HENLEY

enjoyable, interesting, or entertaining. But Emmy's a friend now. I can manage one more appearance at club at least.

As I pass the museum and the playground, I see the usual group in the grassy area where the club practices. Aaron, Nisha, Jude, and some of the others are warming the dogs up. But no Stevie or Bean.

Jude throws a disc in a particularly long, smooth flight pattern, and Meadow catches it with ease. She really is a phenomenal athlete. Bean can be, too, if Stevie keeps working with her. I guess I won't be around to see it.

Emmy spots me walking up and comes over. She hugs me, then studies my face. "Wow, Logan, do you feel okay? I mean this in the most caring of ways, but you look awful."

I laugh shakily. "I'm not great. But to be honest, I don't want to talk about it right now. What's the good news? I could use some right now."

Emmy glances over her shoulder at Jude, then lowers her voice. "It worked! Our plan worked, and especially Saturday night's ruse. Jude came over on Sunday and we talked for hours. He admitted he has feelings for me, but he didn't want to tell me and possibly mess up our friendship. Seeing me with you Saturday night, though, forced him to realize he had to tell me or risk losing having a chance with me. I came clean with him about us and . . . long story short, we're going to give dating a try."

Even though jealousy pulses through my gut, I high five her. "That's great news, Emmy. I'm proud of us."

"Me, too!"

"But what about Stevie? Has he told her?"

Emmy nods. "He said he called her on Monday and let her know. She seemed fine, *relieved* was his word. I checked in with her yesterday to make sure we were okay."

I didn't know any of this. Because Stevie and I aren't talking. Is she going to shut me out entirely? Forever? Because if I'd known that, I never would have given her that note.

"Is she coming tonight?" I ask carefully.

Emmy frowns. "I'm not sure. I didn't hear from her today."

Jude sees me then. He walks over, disc in hand and Meadow prancing by his side. He bumps my fist and puts an arm around Emmy, and then smirks. "Hey, Logan. I hear you're a half-decent actor."

I manage to smile. "Half-decent is right. Emmy's the real talent here."

He laughs. "I don't know. That green dress is a rising star. Seeing it on you," he looks at Emmy, "with you," he raises an eyebrow at me, "pushed me right over the edge."

It's her turn to smirk. "Then it did its job. I'll be sure to wear it again soon."

"Yeah, do," Jude says and kisses her.

Emmy calls the group together. I look around; still no Stevie or Bean. I relax a little. It's painful enough knowing she's in the house and not talking to me. Having her avoid me here too would only heap on the misery.

"Okay, everyone," Emmy says. "As you all know, we have a special demonstration today. Are you ready? Do you know what you're doing?" The others nod. "Then let's get lined up."

Everyone except Emmy spreads out along the throwing line, discs in hand and dogs at the ready. I stand back to watch, but Emmy waves to me. "Come over beside me, Logan."

I have no idea what they're doing, but curious, I walk over to her. Emmy pulls out a whistle, blows, and Aaron, the first person in line, throws a purple disk. Bear chases, catches, and delivers the frisbee back to Aaron who walks over and hands it to me. I take it hesitantly.

Aaron raises an eyebrow. "Turn it over, bro."

I flip the disc. There, written in black marker on the underside, is the letter *I*.

"Thanks?" I'm confused. What is this?

A grinning Emmy pats me on the shoulder. "Wait." She blows the whistle again.

Nisha throws next. Jack doesn't quite catch the red disc, but he snatches it off the ground and brings it back, dropping it at her feet. She hands it to me.

I flip it over. *You* is written there. My eyes jump to Nisha, then to Emmy and Aaron. They're all beaming. I glance around the field. No one else is around, but my body tingles and electricity runs through my veins. My Stevie-sense hums.

Emmy blows again. Jude steps forward with Meadow and runs through a quick freestyle routine. Meadow runs around him, weaves through his lunging legs a few times, leaps on to his back and then off again, and catches the blue disc he flips to her while she's in the air.

Everyone hoots and claps at her performance. Meadow brings the disc to Emmy at her command, who hands it to me. The word *Logan* is on the back. I stare at the three discs in my hand, then up at the group.

Aaron laughs. "You should see your face, man."

"I. You. Logan?" I say.

"Hang on." Emmy grabs a green disc from the ground and after capturing Meadow's attention, throws it. The border collie catches it in the air and brings it back.

My heart thunders in my chest and sweat runs down my back. It's a pretty mild afternoon, but I feel like I'm running a marathon. Could this be what I think it is?

When Meadow brings me the disc, it says *Too*. Emmy gestures to me to look behind me. When I do, I finally see them. Stevie and Bean.

I. You. Logan. Too.

Stevie smiles at me, tears in her eyes, and walks to the line. Her throw is shaky and doesn't go all that far, but I couldn't care less than less. I only want to know what's written on her yellow frisbee. Bean catches it and trots back with it. She lets Stevie take it.

Slowly, her eyes on me, Stevie brings it to me. And on the back of the disc is the word *Love*.

I hold the discs spread out like a hand of cards. *I. You. Logan. Too. Love.*

"Okay, who switched the discs at the last minute?" Emmy complains. "They *were* in order, Stevie, I promise."

"I did," Stevie says with a small, choked voice. She clears her throat and says to me, touching the yellow disc, "I wanted to give you this one myself. I love you too, Logan. And I want to give us a chance."

As tears roll down her cheeks, I drop the discs, sweep her into my arms and kiss her. Then I hold her against me with the immediate plan to never, ever let her go.

Howling, people snatch the frisbees and throw them into the air like graduation caps. The dogs go wild. One of the discs hits Aaron on the way down.

"Ow!"

But all that is background noise. I see Stevie, feel Stevie, smell Stevie, taste Stevie. Her tears mix with a scent that I associate only with her. Something fresh and unexpected, even though I've known her almost all my life.

"Thank you," I whisper in her ear.

"Thank *you*," she says. "For sticking with me all these years. For being honest. And for giving me time to think. Oh! And I have one more surprise."

She slides down to the ground, leashes Bean, and says to the rest of the group, "We'll be back in a few."

"Take your time," Jude says in a suggestive voice. Emmy rolls her eyes at us, and he kisses her.

Our hands entwined, the way I've wished they could be for months, years, Stevie leads me towards the zoo. We don't say much. I'm overwhelmed by knowing that I can touch her, kiss her, tell her how much I love her. I'm not sure how she's feeling; she might not be sure herself. But we have time. Tons of time. Time for it all to unfold.

I realize after a minute that we're not headed toward the zoo, we're going to Duck Lake. When we get there, Stevie points to the graylag geese—a glorious pair of them now—swimming together. As I watch, one goes underwater after a fish while the other keeps watch.

"She's back. Or he. I'm still not sure. Anyway, they're together."

I hug her to me. "I didn't know. I haven't been able to get myself to run by here for a while. I didn't want to see him alone."

Stevie puts her hands on my face and meets my eyes. "I don't think we should make any promises, Logan. But know this. You mean everything to me. You're my best friend, and you're more than that, too. I love you. It's taken me some time—and a little pep talk from Mom—to figure that out, but I know it now. I feel it." She moves her hands to my chest, and I cover them with my own. "I want to make this work. Still . . . promise me one thing."

"What's that?" I ask.

"That whatever happens, we stay friends. The thing I fear most of all is losing you."

She said we shouldn't make promises, so I don't. But I kiss her, long and deep and with every bit of conviction I have in my heart.

It's a promise in and of itself, and I aim to keep it.

Epilogue

Stevie

"I'm so excited for this weekend. It's going to be epic," I say.

Logan squeezes my hand, the hand he's been holding the whole ride up to the mountains despite the questionable safety of having one hand on the wheel while driving on twisty mountain roads.

"Does anyone still say epic?" he teases.

I shrug and pull down the visor mirror to adjust my red winter beanie on my head. My cheeks are pink, my blue eyes are bright, and my hair frames my face. I look . . . happy.

"Who cares? I declare it will be epic. Epic it will be."

He laughs. "If you say so."

I take an extra second to appreciate my boyfriend, a word it only recently hasn't felt weird to call him. He has a fresh haircut, his face is smoothly shaved, he's wearing a forest green puffer coat that brings out the olive flecks in his eyes, and best of all, he's smiling. More than anything lately, I love seeing him smile.

My own grin is as bright as the December afternoon sun, and my laugh is genuine. I feel almost giddy with happiness, something I can safely say I've rarely been before. But that's life with Logan now.

Okay, maybe not all the time. There was the one fight we had about whose room to sleep in. (His won. Mine is now my office and a guest room.) And we *can* get snippy with each other after a long week. But overall, happiness has been my overwhelming emotion for the last three months since I finally came to my senses and committed to being in a relationship with Logan.

He's been an amazing partner so far. The best I've ever had. He never brings me flowers. He hasn't bought me any jewelry—yet. And we've taken the physical side of things slowly, enjoying every mile of the ride.

But he tells me how much he loves me every morning and every night before we fall asleep, he makes me dinner, he walks Bean when my head is stuck in a project, and on my actual birthday, he'd given me a gift certificate to go skydiving again. "Let's have a do-over," the card had said.

In short, he's wonderful. And I'm having an easier and easier time accepting that this new form of love for him is here to stay.

I peek in the back seat. Bean, curled up on a blanket, lifts her head.

"Doing okay back there, Beanie Weenie?" The end of her tail wags. She's going to have an epic weekend, too.

"So, what are we doing up here again?" Logan asks. "Other than a wedding."

"I sent you the agenda that Amelia emailed."

"Yeah . . . I didn't read it."

I groan. "Me, either. I was hoping you did." I dig in my tote bag. "Hang on, I have it in here."

Despite my best efforts with the thirtieth birthday bucket list, organization has not come easy to me. I'm doing my best, but my desk is a disaster area again, the parts of the house I'm responsible for cleaning could use an enema, and I still work too late when I'm excited about a project. I do floss most nights now, so that's something.

I'm trying, anyway. And best of all, I have that new bucket list I wanted to put together. The one focused on improving *other* people's lives. I'll get to it soon.

I pull the cream and black wedding invitation out. It has a coffee stain on it, and Bean chewed the side of it when it came through the mail slot the day it arrived, but it's still legible.

We're invited to join Travis and Amelia for their wedding ceremony and reception at the Lazy Dog Ranch. And the best part: pets are welcome.

I slide the invite behind the other papers and unfold the information sheet Amelia also mailed about the weekend. There are the requisite hotel options first, then the agenda.

"Okay, tonight there's a casual dinner in the dining hall followed by a campfire with adult bevvies and s'mores."

"Mmm," Logan says.

"Tomorrow morning's breakfast is at our leisure, and then we can choose from several delightful ranch activities like snowshoeing, cross-country skiing, or snuggling by the fire."

"I vote for the fire," Logan says.

"After a snowshoe. Bean needs to get her jiggies out."

He nods. "Good point."

"Then lunch, followed by a sleigh ride or wagon ride depending on the conditions."

"Make that a sleigh ride," Logan says. "Looks like there's enough snow."

I glance out of the window. We'd had a winter storm earlier this week that blanketed Denver in snow and blasted the mountains with two feet of the fluffy stuff. It's beautiful, glinting white and gold in the sunlight on the sides of the hills cupping the two-lane highway we're driving along.

I read on. "We should make sure we're prepared with coats and hats and gloves and all that." I slap my head. "Crap. I forgot Bean's winter boots!" She wears small, waterproof boots to protect her paws when it's snowy. She can hike in them, at least for a few hours, without suffering frosty paws.

"I got them," Logan says.

I lean over and smooch him on the cheek. "Thank you. Have I told you I love you?"

"Not since this morning. I was starting to wonder."

"Geez, needy boy. Well, I still love you." I kiss him again, lingering long enough to let him know I was teasing, then read the rest of the page. "After the sleigh ride, there's time to chill, and the wedding ceremony will be at seven o'clock, followed by the reception. The last thing is a brunch Sunday morning, after which I'm sure the ranch owners will be glad to get rid of all of us."

When Bean had her annual appointment a month ago, Travis and Amelia told me the ranch owners were also clients of their practice. They're cutting them an amazing deal to have the wedding there, hoping to generate positive word of mouth and repeat business. Personally, I can't wait. I've never been to a dude ranch.

"Almost there." Logan points to a sign for Lazy Dog Ranch ahead. Bean jumps to her feet, paws on the center console, and stares out of the windshield.

I shake my head. "I swear she speaks human."

"They say border collies are one of the smartest dog breeds," Logan says, and I laugh.

It's a private joke that we recite every time she does something dumb, like trying to sneak into Rosa's yard. The disc dog club has been an incredible outlet for Bean, and for Logan and me for that matter, but it hasn't dissuaded Bean from harassing the flock next door. I guess the bucket list changes are still sinking in for her, too.

Logan pulls off the highway and onto a slushy dirt road. After bumping our way toward the ranch, the property lays out in front of us. Rustic wood buildings of different sizes, including a grand lodge, sit beside a small stream with a little bridge across it. In the distance, a barn and horse stable perch on a small hill next to a paddock, and all around us majestic mountain peaks stand covered in snow.

Logan whistles as he pulls into the parking spot. "This is incredible."

"I'm so excited, and it's not even Christmas yet!" I squeal as we climb out of the car.

I smile at a couple getting out of their own vehicle a few spots away. The woman is tiny. Her knee-high boots almost touch her long winter coat. She smiles back before lifting a cat carrier out of the backseat.

Uh oh. I whirl back to the car, recognizing the danger too late. Bean bounds out of my open door, sniffs the air, and zeroes in on the cat carrier. She darts over, barking excitedly, and sticks her nose almost into the bars of the carrier. The woman tries to lift the carrier out of Bean's reach, but she has trouble getting it out of Bean's vertical leap range.

I run over and leash my dog, spewing apologies. "I'm so sorry. I wasn't expecting another animal in the parking lot. I should have had her on her leash right away."

"That's okay," the woman says once I get Bean under control. She pushes her glasses up her nose and glances at her cat. "Fluffernutter isn't used to dogs. Cats, yes, but not dogs." She pauses. "I'm Beatrix and this is Sebastian." The guy, dark haired and tan, says hello. "And Fluff, of course. Are you here for the wedding?"

"Yes! Travis and Amelia are finally tying the knot." I bounce on my toes. Logan walks over, and I introduce the three of us.

Beatrix smiles. "It's been a long time coming."

Our heads, Bean's and Fluff's included, swivel at the sound of shrill, excited barking coming from the ranch. Three dachshunds tear out of the lodge doors and sprint toward us.

I hold Bean close and Sebastian takes the cat carrier, holding it high to keep it out of reach as the dogs race around our feet, barking feverishly. I'm thrilled to be here with Logan, but a little worry has crept in now that we're here.

Will this be the romantic weekend that Travis and Amelia deserve . . . or a wedding circus of epic proportions?

THE END

It all started with a girl, a boy, and a pug named Doug.
Get the exclusive Love & Pets prequel for FREE!
(www.aghenley.com/free-books)

Love & Pets Book 7:
Twas the night before Christmas, when all through the house, not a creature was stirring . . . except for one sneaky snake, two poorly pugs, three dastardly dachshunds, four curmudgeonly cats, and a pup peeing on a Christmas tree. *Yep, it's a Love & Pets Christmas.*
Read The Pandemonium of Pets: A Love & Pets Christmas Romance now!

Read Next

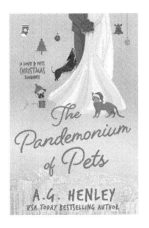

Chapter One
(It's Beginning to Look a Lot Like Christmas)

Travis

Amelia stands in front of the cabin window and looks out over the stunning Colorado mountains. She throws her arms wide as if to embrace the view.

"We're here. We made it. We're actually getting married in this gorgeous place."

I drop our bags on the floor and, puffy coat and winter hat still on, wrap my arms around her from behind. I can't wait to make this woman my wife.

Finally.

She rests her head against my chest. "Some days, I wasn't sure we would."

I kiss the top of her blonde hair. It's soft and smells like some kind of tropical bloom. "I'm sorry it's taken this long."

"It wasn't your fault. It wasn't anyone's fault. We were busy."

That's an understatement.

I'd met Amelia the year of the first annual Love & Pets party —the year my grandmother Jo died. We were engaged by year two, and now, too many years later, we're finally getting married. Tomorrow, to be exact. I tighten my arms around my fiancée.

Outside of the Lazy Dog Ranch's unofficial newlywed cabin, jokingly referred to by the staff as the Hitchin' Post, several feet of powdery snow glitter in the sun thanks to an early season blizzard a week ago. The cabin is a new addition to the ranch, built this past spring. Isa and Addie, clients of ours, had bought the ranch a few years ago, and Isa and her now husband Tobias, the ranch's head wrangler, had met shortly after. Addie and Isa originally shared the original owner's house up the hill, but since Isa and Tobias got married, Addie has her own place in another part of the ranch now.

Down the hill from us, Tobias strides toward the barn and stables, where a few of the ranch's main attractions—the horses —stand in a snow-covered field, blankets on their backs. The equines are the stars at this dude ranch, but Addie, Isa, and Tobias make the place what it is: a warm and welcoming family vacation spot. They'd been great to work with as we planned this holiday wedding shindig.

Amelia turns and presses herself up on her toes to kiss me. "I can't imagine a more blissful setting to exchange our vows."

Her blue-green eyes never fail to capture me; eyes that I've loved for years, through the happiest of times and the hardest.

Together, we'd built our Love & Pets veterinary practice to be the most successful mobile clinic in Colorado, and we're expanding soon to a second vehicle. We have more patients than we know what to do with, many of whom are arriving today to join in the festivities. But Amelia had also been there for me when I'd lost Jo, my only real family. That was one of the roughest times in my life.

"We could have signed the legal paperwork any old day." I'd offered to many times, in fact, so that we didn't have to wait to be married.

"I'm so glad we didn't. Now, we can afford to have a big, beautiful wedding, lots of guests, and all the wonderful memories it will bring for years to come."

I caress her pink cheek, her fleecy hair, her long neck. My hand trails to her shoulders, then to her back, and I pull her against me. As my lips find hers, a whine drags our attention away.

"What is it, Doug?" Amelia asks. One of our two pugs lies in the crate we'd brought, his head on his paws. "I don't think he's feeling well," Amelia says frowning. "He didn't eat well yesterday or today, and I haven't seen him poop in a while."

When you work with animals like we do, talking about poop in the same breath as a kiss comes with the territory.

Daisy, our other pug, licks her snowy paws beside Doug, her stomach bulging. "Looks like Daisy might be snarfing his food."

Amelia snorts. "I wouldn't be surprised if he offers it to her on a silver platter."

I laugh. Dougie is an adoring romantic partner—if you can call a neutered male and spayed female romantic partners.

"We can take a look at him in a minute," I say. "But I'm not quite finished here." I bring her body into mine again, enjoying the way we fit together in all the right places.

I wasn't being noble before. As much as I'm looking forward

157

to our long-awaited celebration with friends and family, I could do without any of the pomp and circumstance this weekend. I just want Amelia to be my wife.

Now. This minute. Yesterday. Always.

I press my lips to hers again with more urgency, lift her off of her feet, and move toward the bed—when the door slams open. The dogs leap to their feet.

"I mean it. If you tell Amelia that, I will never speak to you again."

Avery, Amelia's older sister, backs into the room holding a bucket of champagne and a plate of chocolate-covered strawberries wrapped in plastic. She's petite with short blonde hair and, currently, an angry expression on her face.

Avery is followed by their mother, Joyce, a thin woman who looks like an older version of Amelia: blonde, fair, and small-boned. But that's where the similarity ends between my fiancée and her parent, in my experience.

"I just think she's *crazy* to be getting married, after what we all went through at your father's hands."

Amelia withers, like a flower exposed to its first frost. I put an arm around her and clear my throat. Avery whirls at the sound.

"Oh! We thought you two would already be down at the lodge. Well, that's one surprise ruined." She holds up the bucket and plate and then sets them on a small table near the cabin's mini kitchen. "Happy day before your wedding!"

"Thank you very much," I say. "How are you today, Joyce?"

Joyce's eyes narrow and her lips thin. I can practically sniff out her disapproval from across the room. It smells a lot like expensive perfume. "I'm fine. Thank you, Travis." She turns her attention to her younger daughter. "Amelia, you aren't planning to wear *that* tonight, are you?"

"I, well . . ." She looks down at her white sweater, dark jeans, and cowboy boots, and shrivels a little more. "It's only a casual barbecue for our guests, Mom."

Avery's eyes flash at their mother. "You look gorgeous, Melly. Love that outfit."

Joyce ignores her older daughter. "Well, you could have made a bit more effort. And you'll drip sauce all over that top. Mark my words."

Daisy sniffs Joyce's pant leg suspiciously, and Joyce pushes her —not hard, but still—out of her way with her foot to get to the fridge, where she stores the wine and berries.

Amelia and Avery's eyes lock, speaking volumes behind their mother's back. None of the volumes are complimentary. I haven't had the . . . pleasure . . . of spending much time with Joyce over the years. A holiday here or there, and a few visits from her that Amelia mostly tried to shield me from. But I haven't needed a lot of time to take her measure.

"So, Amelia, is Dad coming?" Avery asks her sister pointedly. Amelia winces.

Joyce whirls. "Michael's coming? I thought he wasn't coming!"

Amelia shrugs meekly. "I'm not sure. You know Dad."

"I can't believe he's coming," Joyce says. "Why did you even invite him, Amelia?"

"Because he's our father, that's why," Avery answers. "And he'll be walking you down the aisle if he does come, right Mel?"

Amelia hems and haws, obviously not wanting to upset her mother. Which is the exact opposite of what Avery's comment was intended to do.

"I'm not sure yet. Kenny offered to escort me, too."

"I love Kenny," Avery says with affection. "He and Ruston were in the lobby checking in before we came up."

"We could walk down," Amelia says to me quickly. "It would be fun to see people as they arrive. More time to visit."

Doug and Daisy rush toward the door, barking, at the word *walk*. Joyce hustles out of their way as if they might give her ticks and fleas in passing.

"Yes, you can go too." Amelia croons to the dogs.

"And another thing. Why on earth did you invite people to bring their pets?" Joyce complains. "You might as well have chosen the zoo as your venue."

This time, Avery looks like she agrees with their mother, even if she won't say so in front of her.

I field this one. "Pets are what we do. They're a huge part of our lives, and we wanted our patients and their owners to be able to share in the fun with us this weekend."

Amelia and I have worked hard to build our business, and we couldn't have done it without the support and referrals of our clients. Inviting them and their pets is a way we can thank them for helping us succeed.

Joyce tosses her shoulder-length hair back. It moves in one fascinating clump. "Ridiculous, if you ask me. But it's your wedding."

Amelia bristles, but I can tell she's not going to argue. She's been working on building some assertiveness with their mother for a long time, but . . . she isn't quite there yet. After snapping a leash on Doug and grabbing her coat, she marches out of the cabin.

With a heavy sigh, her mother follows. And after a sad shake of her head in my direction, Avery leaves, too.

Daisy waits expectantly by her own leash. I move that way. I miss my grandma Jo every single day, so I'm happy to have any and all of Amelia's family members in our lives. But I can't help thinking that Joyce would give any monster-in-law a run for her money.

Families fight and argue at weddings and especially around the holidays, right? If that's true, then . . . it's beginning to look a lot like Christmas.

Read The Pandemonium of Pets: A Love & Pets Christmas Romance now!

Afterword

The Conundrum of Collies, and my choice of border collies as the breed to write about, was inspired by a dog that hasn't been alive for over fourteen years.

Katy was my husband's and my first fur baby, a four-year-old border collie and Australian shepherd mix that we adopted from the no-kill shelter in Boulder, Colorado.

We could tell right away that she was intelligent but wary. We were told she was friendly but didn't like other dogs. We were twenty-two and inexperienced as pet owners, but we just knew she was perfect.

The first night we took Katy home, she bit my face. Just a warning nip. *Uh oh.* Within the first year, she bit my lip, causing me to bleed and leaving a little scar, snapped at the heel of a man walking by (luckily he wore thick cowboy boots), and bit the leg of a boy who unintentionally roller skated into her while playing roller hockey on our street. It wasn't a serious injury, but we felt terrible.

Houston, we had a problem. Other dogs, Katy loved. She didn't trust humans.

We did the best we could as young dog owners. We took her to dog training, which helped her behavior a lot, we kept her on a short leash and away from strangers, ran with her to burn energy, and tried to teach her to catch a frisbee. (She had zero interest—she gave the most withering looks when she felt something was beneath her). We rescued Zippy, a dachshund-terrier mix and our second fur baby, to keep her company. Katy adored Zippy. Zippy loved humans and ignored Katy.

Katy remained wary of people. One night we invited one of my husband's coworkers over for dinner. She sat right by his side all night. He thought she liked him, but we knew better. She was keeping a very close eye on him—just in case. A year or two later, she tore up a square foot of wood flooring when she thought she heard something in the vent below (and maybe she did). Katy and Zippy loved escaping from our yard. One time, like Bean, they ended up in someone's fenced backyard. Luckily, they had their collars and identification tags on and we got a call to pick them up. We kept working with them.

Katy lived to be fifteen. In the last five years, she developed epilepsy, bad hips and knees, and hearing loss. The hearing loss turned out to be a blessing. Once she was deaf, she let down her guard a bit. She slept longer and more soundly. She didn't worry about who might be at the front door or walking by on the other side of the street (or several streets over, for that matter). Things skittering in the vents? Who cares?

When Katy was fourteen, I found her splayed out on her back, snoozing. Normally, when she sensed someone come into the room, she'd jump up, ready to investigate the source of trouble. This time, she popped an eye open, saw it was me, and went back to sleep. It had only taken ten years, but Katy had relaxed.

The last few years, she lived her best life. She smiled a lot (you know dogs can smile, right?), dug in the trash with joyful abandon, and she loved visits from friends and family—canines and humans alike.

When her bad hips and knees finally gave out, no longer holding her weight, she passed away in our living room with Zippy curled up nearby and my husband and me by her side, petting her until her eyes closed for the last time. She was at peace.

Okay, there was that time at age thirteen when she chewed up and swallowed part of a rib bone and had to have several inches of her pierced intestines removed in emergency surgery, only by then we'd learned.

No dog is perfect.

But Katy was ours. And we loved her.

A.G. Henley, September 2020

Acknowledgments

I can't believe the Love & Pets series has grown to six books! Each one has been so much fun to write. I love to hear from readers about which is their favorite, and which breed they think I should write about next. You, dear readers, make the long hours at my desk worth it. Thank you for buying, reading, reviewing, and telling others about my books.

Speaking of reviews, special thanks to the Henley Huddle, my review team. I appreciate each and every one of you. The Love & Pets Facebook group has also been very helpful when I get stuck thinking of book titles, or when I need to find out if most people would know what a disc dog club is.

Many thanks to Lorie Humpherys for her proofreading prowess. If someone can read a book as quickly and carefully as she, I've yet to meet them. I'm also grateful to Najla Qamber and her team at Najla Qamber Designs for their eye catching, colorful covers. Super readers and book-loving friends Kathy Azzolina and Terri White keep me laughing with their memes and messages.

Finally, love and thanks to all of my family and friends. Your support means everything.

Also by A. G. Henley

The Love & Pets Series (Sweet Romantic Comedy)

Love, Pugs, and Other Problems: A Love & Pets Prequel Story

The Problem with Pugs

The Trouble with Tabbies

The Downside of Dachshunds

The Lessons of Labradors

The Predicament of Persians

The Conundrum of Collies

The Pandemonium of Pets: A Love & Pets Christmas Romance

The Love & Pets Series Box Set: Books 1 - 3

Nicole Rossi Thrillers (Young Adult)

Double Black Diamond

The Brilliant Darkness Series (Young Adult Fantasy)

The Scourge

The Keeper: A Brilliant Darkness Story

The Defiance

The Gatherer: A Brilliant Darkness Story

The Fire Sisters

The Brilliant Darkness Boxed Set

Novellas (Young Adult Fantasy)

Untimely

Featured in *Tick Tock: Seven Tales of Time*

Basil and Jade

Featured in *Off Beat: Nine Spins on Song*

The Escape Room

Featured in *Dead Night: Four Fits of Fear*

About the Author

A.G. Henley is a *USA Today* bestselling author of novels and stories in multiple genres including thrillers, romantic comedies, and fantasy romances. The first book in her young adult Brilliant Darkness series, *The Scourge*, was a Library Journal Self-e Selection and a Next Generation Indie Book Award finalist. She's also a clinical psychologist, but she promises not to analyze you . . . much.

Find her at:
aghenley.com
Email Aimee

Made in the USA
Middletown, DE
26 September 2023

39428094R00106